THE
BEGINNING

THE BEGINNING
WITH GROUP STUDY GUIDE

ROBERT MEYER

Tate Publishing & *Enterprises*

The Beginning
Copyright © 2011 by Robert Meyer. All rights reserved.

No part of this publication may be reproduced, stored in a retrieval system or transmitted in any way by any means, electronic, mechanical, photocopy, recording or otherwise without the prior permission of the author except as provided by USA copyright law.

The opinions expressed by the author are not necessarily those of Tate Publishing, LLC.

Published by Tate Publishing & Enterprises, LLC
127 E. Trade Center Terrace | Mustang, Oklahoma 73064 USA
1.888.361.9473 | www.tatepublishing.com

Tate Publishing is committed to excellence in the publishing industry. The company reflects the philosophy established by the founders, based on Psalm 68:11,
"The Lord gave the word and great was the company of those who published it."

Book design copyright © 2011 by Tate Publishing, LLC. All rights reserved.
Cover design by Kristen Verser
Interior design by Leah LeFlore

Published in the United States of America

ISBN: 978-1-61777-014-2
1. Religion, Christian Church, Growth   2. Religion, Christian Life, Devotional
11.03.10

DEDICATION

This book is dedicated to my wife, Melanie, for her non-stop encouragement in all I do. And to my daughters, Joanna and Kirsten, from whom I have learned so much. And to the many churches that have endured my fumbling attempts to turn into reality the passion the Lord has placed in my heart for a vibrant, growing church.

TABLE OF CONTENTS

9 • Foreword
11 • Introduction
13 • Prologue

WEEK ONE

17 • The Partners
25 • Serve Me
33 • Keep Me Safe
41 • Do My Bidding

WEEK TWO

51 • Teach Me Bible Facts
59 • Let's Have Fun
65 • Stir My Emotions
71 • Let's Be Holier

WEEK THREE

81 • Let Someone Else Do It
87 • Help Someone Else Do the Work
91 • Only Our Kind
97 • Out of Step

WEEK FOUR

109 • Non-essentials
115 • Worshiping Our History
123 • What Have We Learned?
139 • What Do We Do Next?

WEEK FIVE

147 • Evangelism
165 • Walking by Faith
179 • New Values for Christians
189 • Follow the Leader

WEEK SIX

203 • Cultural Relevancy
213 • Repentance
223 • Prayer
231 • The Beginning of the End, or the End of the Beginning?

245 • How to Use the Study Guide
249 • Endnotes
251 • Bibliography

FOREWORD

THE CHURCH IN NORTH AMERICA, ALONG WITH THE CHURCH IN EUROPE AND AUSTRALIA AND NEW ZEALAND, IS DYING. The three continents most touched by the Protestant Reformation find themselves at odds with the rest of the world in terms of new converts and growth.

The Beginning, by Robert Meyer, approaches this problem not in a didactic way but in a narrative format. He clearly articulates the elephants in the living room for most congregations. However, he then offers hope by showing congregations how they again can obey their Lord, experience health, and begin to grow by making many more disciples for Jesus Christ.

In this culture, "story" is king. Therefore, I am hoping that many pastors, elders, deacons, and other lay people will read the narrative in this book. For by doing so, they will be confronted with how many of their congregations are living a theology that is disobedient to God's intention for the church of Jesus Christ. But in reading the narrative they will also realize there is hope. The same hope we have experienced in Growing Healthy Churches in northern California and northwest Nevada, where in five years we saw God help us go from thirty-seven growing congregations to one hundred and fifty-three healthy growing congregations. We watched older, established congregations not only change but become evangelistic entities that today are constantly producing new disciples for Jesus Christ.

Robert Meyer's story is really God's story of hope for a nation filled with congregations that need repentance and guidance in how to become the congregations God designed them to be.

—Dr. Paul D. Borden
Executive Minister, Growing Healthy Churches
Author of *Hit the Bullseye*, *Direct Hit*, and *Assaulting the Gates*

INTRODUCTION

I HAVE WRITTEN THIS BOOK OUT OF A DEEP PASSION TO SEE THE CHURCH IN AMERICA COME AWAKE. As soon as I accepted Christ as my Savior at the age of seventeen, the Lord began to burn into my DNA an urgent hunger to see the church thrive and be effective in reaching others.

This book is written as fiction out of a desire that it will be read by large numbers of people in the church. It isn't written to be read just by pastors and church leaders. My great desire is that it will have a profound effect on all the people in our churches.

It is a story of what is happening in far too many of the Christian churches in America. While the characters and churches in this book are fictional representations of real people and churches, the facts presented are not fiction. I wish they were, but they are not. It is my prayer that this book is not just another work of fiction. My prayer is that it will become reality.

In my work with churches, an amazing thing has been happening. We are starting to see the things written about in this novel taking place in churches. This work of fiction is starting to come true! But there is so much more to be done! I call on Christians everywhere to pray that the Lord will bring a great awakening of the church in America. Please pray and get to work making these changes in your church and everywhere you can be of influence.

If used prayerfully, intentionally, and in the way it was designed to be used, this book can be an instrument of the Lord to bring transformation to your congregation. Guidance regarding how to use the study guide is given at the end of the book in the "How to Use the Study Guide" chapter.

PROLOGUE

"I THINK THEY'RE DYING!" lamented Rick.

"It's scary to watch the signs of life fade before our eyes," agreed Wayne.

"I'm so tired of feeling the utter frustration of not knowing how to help," Al chimed in.

The couple sitting at the table near them at the local Chili's leaned in to better hear the conversation, giving each other concerned looks and wondering who was dying.

Rick went on, "I'm awakened many nights by the feelings of hopelessness. That heavy feeling in the pit of my stomach has been my alarm clock far too often lately."

"This sounds really tragic," whispered the woman at the next table to her husband.

"What I don't understand," Al joined in, "is *why* so many churches are doing so poorly."

"Churches?" mumbled the husband, almost choking on the piece of pie in his mouth.

"I'm beginning to wonder whether I've made a mistake in accepting the responsibility of being superintendent. Frustration has been my constant companion for the three years I've been in this position. I have a heart for my denomination, but," Rick confessed, "I'm always wondering what I am doing wrong? I feel like a phenomenal failure."

Wayne nodded. Rick went on, "I'm responsible for the life, health, and growth of the seventy-eight churches in my region. But, with rare exception, these churches are not alive and healthy, and they certainly are not growing. In fact, of the seventy-eight churches I oversee, only four are growing at all. The rest are either shrinking or pretty much just chugging along like they have for the last ten years. The ones that are shrinking make up the greatest number of all."

"It's the same with the churches in my region," added Wayne. "The churches I pastored myself seemed to thrive. They grew rapidly with many people coming to Christ. Why am I not able to help the churches in this region have a similar experience?"

The lady nodded knowingly at her husband. "Sounds like our church. People just seem different nowadays. I think we're just too busy anymore, trying to make it in this economy, to feel like getting involved. Maybe that's why they think their churches are dying." Her husband gave her a glance that said, *Let's keep listening and find out.*

Al empathized. "It had seemed so easy when I was leading the church. But it's more difficult than I ever imagined to inspire the congregations in my region to wake up and live the adventure that I know God has purposed for them. Walking with the Lord should be the most exciting life ever! Why are so many Christians so complacent?"

It didn't help for the trio to realize that most of the other regional superintendents of their particular denomination were experiencing similar frustrations. Actually, it seemed that most of them had just accepted that this was the way it was and always would be. They had accommodated to this reality and had chosen to be content in a care-taking role, even if that meant that their churches were on a path to death. They had managed to ignore the reality that many of these churches would be closing their doors soon. Somehow they had found a way to not let that bother them.

Rick and his two colleagues had not yet managed to make this accommodation. Seeing the church in decline ate away at their souls.

WEEK ONE

THE PARTNERS

RICK, AL, AND WAYNE HAD MANAGED TO FIND EACH OTHER DURING THE LAST YEAR. At the regional superintendents' meetings, they had come to realize that they shared a common frustration over the ugly state of the church in America. They found themselves eating meals together, taking walks together, and staying up at night to talk about their concerns. Then they began phoning and e-mailing each other between meetings. They were searching for a solution to the problem that had been consuming them separately for the last few years. It was comforting to each of them to realize that they were not alone in this struggle, but they had not yet found any solutions to their problems.

They began to read the same books and journal articles. In one way it was comforting to know that they were not alone. But it was shocking to learn that 94 percent of churches in America were either at a plateau or declining.[1] Something was seriously wrong here!

Each of these three superintendents had a similar life story. Each had come to faith in Jesus during their high school years. Upon making this decision to give their lives to the Lord, they had been filled with a passion for the life and health of the church. None of them had planned on being a pastor. They had each chosen another career path. But through their college years, they became more and more involved in the Lord's work until it seemed a logical path to pursue the ministry full time. For each, the burning in their souls to see the church flourish gradually came to take first place in their lives. Soon it seemed the most natural thing in the world to put other plans aside to prepare for ministry.

Upon graduation from seminary, they had accepted the call to their first churches. They soon realized that in seminary they had really only been given some tools that would allow them to prepare, on their own, to become effective pastors. They did not yet have the skills to lead a church effectively. One thing they each did have, however, was a passion for reaching lost people with the gospel. As they fumbled through the first few years of ministry, the one thing all three had in common was that people were coming to faith in Jesus in their churches and these congregations were growing.

Other pastors sometimes looked at them like they were an oddity and even manifested jealousy at the "success" they were having. They didn't think of it as success at all. To them it was just the way it was supposed to be in the church. To them, the churches that were *not* growing were the oddity. They continued to pursue their passion and learned even more about how to effectively reach lost people, and as a consequence, the churches they pastored grew even more rapidly. But as so often happens, they ended up being "promoted" to the greater responsibility of regional superintendent. And that is where the rub came in.

Now they were responsible for not just leading one church but, in Rick's case, seventy-eight churches. Al and Wayne had a similar workload. And they all had a similar frustration. Leading one church to reach unreached people and grow numerically had seemed such a natural thing when they were the pastors of those churches. Now that they were not the pastor of any church, but in reality, the pastor to a bunch of pastors, it wasn't so simple. In fact, it was proving to be incredibly frustrating for all three of them. They kept asking each other, "What can we do to get these churches going?"

Their wives, Marilyn, Janis, and Chloe, began to worry about them. This was taking such an emotional toll on the men that it affected their relationships at home. They were not getting enough sleep. They grumped at their wives and children. It got to the point that their wives wondered if their husbands should not go back to being the pastor of just one church. Their husbands had seemed much happier then, and life was so much simpler in that role. This all seemed to be leading to a not very happy conclusion.

Fortunately, these three superintendents had each other. They could share their burden with one another; they could begin to learn together. And learn they did. They began to share stories with each other of the churches they were responsible for. As they did, they noticed some patterns beginning to emerge.

They also began to study the church at large in America. The more they learned, the more concerned they became. The church in their country was indeed in serious straits. Not only were 94 percent of churches in America either stagnant in their attendance or losing attendees, but things were actually worse than this. The scariest thing they learned was the decline in numbers of people accepting Christ. During the World War II generation's prime, 65 percent of their fellow citizens accepted Christ as their Savior. In their own generation, the Baby Boomers, only 35 percent of the population made that decision. For their children, the Baby Busters, only 15 percent made that decision. In the most recent generation, sometimes called the Digitals, only 4 percent of the population had accepted Christ.[2] They had all heard and believed that if any generation failed to win its generation to faith in the Lord, the church would disappear. They began to realize how perilously close to that day the church was coming.

They began to wonder, *What happened to the days when, in spite of great opposition and persecution, the church turned the world upside down?*

In the first century, Christians faced the real possibility of losing their life for sharing their faith. But they continued to spread the good news so intensely and effectively that so many people accepted Christ that Christianity was adopted as the official religion of the Roman Empire. This occurred in the most powerful nation on earth, which controlled most of the known world and, at first, savagely persecuted Christians. This took place in a nation in which worship of the emperor was, for most, the predominant religion. How safe would these people feel in supplanting worship of the emperor with worship of this radical Jesus? In spite of all this, the gospel spread powerfully. They started asking, *Does God have less power today than he did in that day? Is he any less willing to send that power into our lives now than he was then? Has he failed to keep his promise, "All authority in heaven and on earth has been given to me. Therefore, go and make disciples...And surely I am with you always, to the very end of the age"?* (Matthew 28:18-20).

The answer to these questions was clearly a resounding *no*. They realized that the problem then must be with those who call themselves Christians.

Why are we, who claim to serve the Lord, so ineffective in fulfilling his primary mission on earth? They wondered. *We certainly cannot blame it on persecution or any way in which we have suffered for naming the name of Jesus. We certainly cannot blame it on lack of opportunity or resources.*

They began to think, *We who have lived in America during the last two hundred years have had the greatest opportunity for the spread of the gospel in the history of the human race. Until now, our government has favored Christianity and passed laws making it easier for churches to operate. Until the last generation, most of our citizens have had a generally favorable opinion of Christians. No people in the history of the human race have enjoyed such economic freedom and prosperity. All of these could have been used in the spread of the gospel. But we have squandered that opportunity. As a consequence, the church is losing ground all through our nation. About six percent of our churches are growing in attendance, but, of these growing churches, some are growing purely by attracting Christians who used to attend the churches that are now declining. This transfer growth is not real growth for the kingdom. It is simply moving sheep from one pen to another, not increasing the size of the flock. The number of churches that are growing significantly through the conversion of lost people to faith in Jesus Christ is probably no more than three percent of the churches in this country.*

They thought about the fact that, in addition to these few growing largely by transfer growth, there are those churches that are growing by presenting a false gospel, a gospel that has no place in its theology for suffering of any kind, a gospel that falsely claims that if we "just have faith" all our problems will be instantly solved. They had each, at times, commented "It is easy to attract large numbers of people with such teaching. But that teaching misleads people. It does not accurately reflect what the Lord of the universe has told us in his word." They knew that over and over again God uses suffering as part of his process of maturing, pruning, and bringing his followers to a place of complete dependence on him rather than on themselves and their clever strategies. Rick said, "A church that never teaches that God will bring some hardships into the life of every believer fails to teach the whole counsel of God. It is easy to attract a large crowd with such incomplete teaching, but such teaching will leave those who follow it desperate when not all of their problems are solved right away."

When they added up all these factors, it was easy to see why the church in this country was in such bad shape. Christians were not winning large numbers of people to faith in Jesus. They were, for the most part, not equipping Christians to be world changers. They had all seen that disobedience to such a central command of our Lord resulted in weak Christians and weak churches.

They had each led churches that had reached lost people in significant numbers but those churches represented such a tiny fraction of the total number of churches. They reached such a tiny percentage of the whole population. Those few bright spots did not alleviate the fact that the overall picture was very dark indeed.

One of the most telling realities for them was that so few of the children who were raised in Bible-teaching churches stayed faithful to the Lord once they got away from home. One day Al fumed to the others, "I just heard that currently only about 9 percent of children who are raised in Christian homes continue to be involved in the practice of their faith after they graduate from high school![3] That means 91 percent walk away from Christianity upon leaving home. Even if those numbers are not absolutely accurate, even if twice that percentage stay true to the Lord, it is still a horrifying number of Christian young people who chuck it all overboard once they leave home. Something is desperately wrong with the church when even the children who were raised in its embrace abandon it as soon as they are on their own!"

They had wondered why so few of their churches had any significant numbers of twenty-somethings in attendance. Now they understood. If only 4 percent of that generation were accepting Christ, and if only 9 percent of those raised in the church were staying with it upon leaving home, there simply weren't enough Christians in that generation to represent any significant percentage of their churches.

They also began to realize why the church was having so little impact in American culture. Together they had prayed about why the culture around them was becoming so anti-Christian. It began to make sense. In their culture Christianity was regarded as, at best, irrelevant. The gospel was not making any difference in the lives of the vast majority of their population. Of course most people regarded it as irrelevant. Most had never heard an accurate presentation of the gospel. What they had heard and seen was the distorted representation of Christianity presented by the news media.

They saw the media representing Christianity as a threat to the American way of life. Even their own government, in a document prepared by the Homeland Security Department, classified returning veterans and conservative Christians as one of the greatest terrorism concerns. They watched their churches struggle with increasing governmental controls. Over and over again churches were being told they couldn't build on land they had purchased, or they couldn't expand their building on their current site. Or they were being told they had to build their church buildings in industrial zones where the land was outrageously expensive, or they would be limited to five acres of land at the most. The Religious Land Use and Institutionalized Persons Act, passed by Congress, forbids local jurisdictions from doing this, but most of their churches were unaware of their rights in this matter. They just gave up as soon as the city or county told them *no* in one form or another.

Rick, Al, and Wayne were startled to learn that, while Christianity was in serious decline, Islam had, in the minds of some, become the fastest growing religion in America. No one could deny that there had been a tremendous rise in the influence of Islam in their country. Over and over again they saw their government, including their president, bend over backwards to present Islam in the most positive light possible.

They were also becoming increasingly concerned about the growing suspicion and even hostility toward Christians that they saw manifested throughout their culture. A surprising number of seemingly average, ordinary citizens were beginning to regard Christianity with real suspicion. Far too many people had come to regard

Christianity as the source of many of their problems. They were suspicious of Christians in general. They were afraid that if Christianity were allowed to have its way, it would take away from them many of the things they had come to hold dear. Wayne, especially, because of his studies in history, realized that this was a radical departure from the cultural climate of fifty years ago. How had this come to be?

These three men of God realized it would be so easy to blame "those others" for the decline of Christianity and the rise of an anti-Christian culture. But they were honest enough to admit that the reason for these woes was that Christians had failed to do their job. Wayne mused, "If the church had been winning millions of people to faith in Jesus during the last one hundred years, things would be very different. When Jesus is invited to be the Lord of a life he transforms that life. When millions of lives are changed by God, it changes the culture." They knew that only those who know the power of the gospel to change people can change a culture for good. They agonized over the fact that the church had failed to fulfill the central mandate it had been given. Two questions disturbed them the most. How did the church get to this point of weakness and ineffectiveness? And how could it get out of this mess?

They began to pray and study together trying to find answers and solutions. They began to look carefully at the churches they were responsible for. They wanted to understand in very personal terms what had gone wrong in these churches they were beginning to know so well. They began to study their churches and read everything they could on church health and growth.

QUESTIONS FOR REFLECTION

1. Is your church among the 94 percent of churches in America that are not growing or the 6 percent that are growing?

2. Why do you think your church is in its current condition?

SERVE ME

TRINITY CHURCH WAS ESPECIALLY FRUSTRATING TO AL. He just couldn't figure out what was wrong there.

They had recently built a beautiful new building on a major local carrier road, and were located in a rapidly growing suburb of a major metropolitan area. There were many reachable people in their immediate area. But they continued to just trudge along. They had shown a small initial spurt of growth upon opening up the new building, but that only lasted for a few months. Soon they had reverted to their previous stagnant ways. *Why would a church in such a favorable situation exhibit no growth?* Al was puzzled.

Then Al remembered a comment made to him by the chairman of the church shortly after the new building was opened. He had expressed concern that "all these new people are becoming members, and we are going to lose control of the church!" That comment had frustrated Al tremendously when he first heard it, and he couldn't quite understand what would motivate a leader in this congregation to make such a remark. Then he remembered the results of some research done several decades ago by Win Arn of the Institute for American Church Growth. Arn had surveyed the membership of one thousand churches. One of the questions he had asked them was, "Why does the church exist?"

At that time 89 percent of the respondents had said, "The church exists to take care of me and my family." More recent research by George Barna suggests that the number giving that same response is now up to 91 percent.[4]

Al was astounded by these research results. But they did explain the comment made by the Trinity Church chairman. *Apparently 91 percent of American Christians today believe that the reason the church is there is all about them. It exists to keep them happy, entertained, safe, and to solve all their problems for them. They have assumed that God has committed himself to making their lives easy, fulfilling, and free of anything hard,* Al thought.

He began to understand. A consumer mentality had overrun the churches to such an extent that the vast majority of Christians now saw their role in the church as that of consumer of the services provided by the church. He realized that sometimes the pastors themselves fostered this thinking. He remembered one executive pastor who stood before the congregation and proclaimed, "We are here to serve you." In the consumer oriented society in which Rick, Al, and Wayne lived, that didn't seem like such an outrageous comment. Only in the light of the huge consumer mentality that had filled the churches did he see that comment as adding to the problem by furthering the mentality that the church exists to serve its members.

Trinity Church was not growing by reaching lost people because the people themselves did not want the church to grow. They were convinced the church was to be focused on their "needs." Never mind that most of what they called "needs" were really just desires for safety, comfort, pleasure, coddling, ego stroking, and entertainment. They had not gotten the message the Lord gave in Ephesians 4:11-12 that : "He gave some to be pastors and teachers, to prepare God's people for works of service..." It never entered their minds that maybe the church existed to train them to become effective servants of God. They wanted to be served, not to serve.

Of course, if one thinks the church exists to serve him or her there is no thought given to reaching others with the gospel. That would require sacrifice on the part of the people. They would have to give up their comfort zone. They might be embarrassed if someone snickered at them as they attempted to share their faith. Who knows? There was even a slight possibility that someone would be rude to them. There was zero possibility that they would be put to death for sharing their faith. They would not be burned at the stake or fed to the lions in the arena or experience being beheaded like those who had gone before them in the faith. But who wants to be embarrassed?

Al came to realize that evangelism had not been the first priority at Trinity Church. In fact, if he were honest about it, it certainly wasn't even among the top ten priorities in this congregation. Oh, there was some occasional lip service given to outreach, but that was as far as it ever got. No sacrifices were made to see that outreach occurred. All decisions made by the church were motivated by only the desires of the existing congregation. No thought was given in the preparation of the annual budget to funding activities that would reach people who needed the Lord. All programming decisions were made with a desire to please those who were already in the church. Every Sunday service was planned only with an eye to the audience of those who were already Christians and comfortably ensconced in their pews. They were, after all, the "consumers" of the services they had paid for with their 2.5 percent "tithes" to the church, and they deserved to be taken care of in the manner to which they had grown accustomed. If they only showed up one or two Sundays per month, that was "the best they could do." What difference did it make if they were not there consuming the services of the church every Sunday? The church existed to serve them. How dare anyone suggest that maybe, just maybe, they had it all backwards, that maybe the church was there to train them to be effective servants of the living and almighty God?

There was another problem that Al recognized. *There are quite a few people in these churches who are using the church to inflate their ego*, he mused. *They feel like they don't amount to much in their life outside the church, but in the church they are big fish in a small pond. Teaching a Sunday school class, being an elder, leading worship, or doing the announcements gives them recognition and an ego boost. And they don't want anyone intruding on their turf. They cling to their position of prestige, influence, and even power, as though it is a matter of life and death. No wonder they don't want anything to change. If new people come into the church, it is a threat to the little nest they have carefully lined for themselves.*

Al kept getting an uncomfortable feeling. *One of the main reasons the churches in my care are not growing is that the people don't want the churches to grow. They really don't care whether their friends, neighbors, relatives, or work associates go to hell. What they really care about is being able to go to church to be entertained, pampered, coddled, and served! If a bunch of new people become Christians, these pampered church members might actually have to serve someone else instead of themselves. That would never do! It was already a huge inconvenience to have to work in the nursery one Sunday a month taking care of their own children! Someone else should be doing that for them so they can sit as consumers in the church service without having to put forth any effort beyond singing and raising their hands.*

He also began to realize that at least some of the mega churches in his metro area were growing because they simply could offer more services to the consumer Christians who had come to be the vast majority of people in the churches. These churches were simply outcompeting the smaller churches in the rush to provide more entertainment and services to consumer oriented Christians.

The sad part of this mentality is that it didn't satisfy the people. They were left empty and frustrated because they were ignoring a reality that is absolutely clear in the Scriptures. The way to joy is to lose ourselves in obedience to the Lord. Jesus himself said in Matthew 6:31-33,

> So do not worry, saying, "What shall we eat?" or "What shall we drink?" or "What shall we wear?" for the pagans run after all these things, and your heavenly Father knows that you need them. But seek first his kingdom and his righteousness and all these things will be given to you as well.

Al had frequently used two charts when he preached on this subject in his own church.

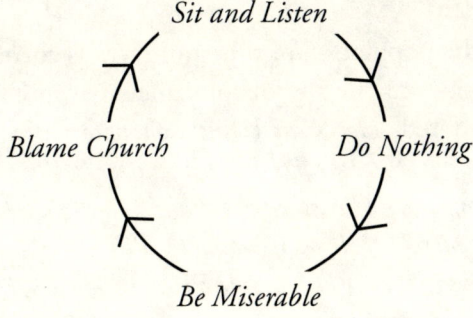

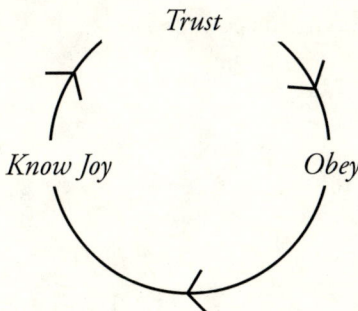

The charts pointed out that only when we give ourselves to trusting the Lord's promises and obeying His commands can we find fullness of joy. By clinging to their own lives, the people of Trinity Church were, in reality, losing them.

Of course the selfishness manifested by the consumer-driven mentality meant that there were significant divisions in the church. When everyone was looking out for their own self-interest, squabbles inevitably arose. The problem was that other people had other desires that they called "their needs." Often the desires of one person were in direct opposition to the desires of the other. It was, of course, impossible for the church to do two opposite things at the same time, so someone was going to be frustrated. Someone was going to think that the church was failing in its God-given responsibility to take care of them. So, sure enough, there was a lot of squabbling in Trinity Church. In fact, the church was gaining quite a reputation in their area for the internecine warfare that took place in the congregation.

Al sadly faced the fact that the number one reason why only 4 percent of the population of this country was currently being won to faith in Christ was the rise of consumer-driven Christianity.

Al wondered, *How can I ever motivate pastors to motivate their people to change their hearts in this matter? What will it take to get American consumer Christians to realize that they have a much higher calling than merely their own comfort? Will it require that the Lord take away the comforts that these people have so come to rely on? Will it require that Christians face genuine persecution for their faith?*

Al quietly began to pray that God would act powerfully to awaken his people in this country.

QUESTIONS FOR REFLECTION

1. Is there any evidence of the "consumer mentality" in your church?
2. How is that affecting your church?

KEEP ME SAFE

WHEN RICK THOUGHT ABOUT BETHEL CHURCH IT MADE HIM WANT TO LEAVE HIS POSITION AS SUPERINTENDENT. Actually it made him want to stomp around shouting! *What a frustrating church! How many sticks of dynamite would it take to blast this church out of the concrete rut it had made for itself?* The people of the church had elevated caution to the highest level of art form. They had made "the voice of reason" the godliest of attributes. Every time anyone in the church proposed any action that involved the slightest bit of risk, the graybeards of the congregation would respond, "We need to be careful," "All things need to be done decently and in order," and, "We don't want to run ahead of God."

Amazingly, the congregation had come to accept that this attitude was the highest of virtues. They kept electing elders who were cautious in the extreme. In one way, this was understandable. The men never urged the congregation to take scary steps of faith. Everyone could dwell in their safe little world without ever taking any significant risk. It sure was a lot easier to live this way.

But, thought Rick, *there is a problem with this philosophy. It is exactly the opposite of the way God, in the Scriptures, has instructed us to live. In Hebrews 11:1 we are told, "Now faith is being sure of what we hope for and certain of what we do not see." In other words, faith means we are not able to count, measure, see, or experience with any of our physi-*

cal senses that which we believe will happen. We believe it because God promised in Ephesians 3:20 to "do immeasurably more than all we ask or imagine, according to His power that is at work within us." We don't believe it because there is some human way to measure it. We believe it because we are trusting God to do what seems humanly impossible.

Rick reflected that living this way was the only way to please God. He remembered that Hebrews 11:6 says, "Without faith it is impossible to please God, because anyone who comes to him must believe that he exists and that he rewards those who earnestly seek him." The examples given in Hebrews 11 are all examples of people who trusted God to do that which was humanly impossible.

In verse 7, the example given is of Noah. Rick could just picture how God came to Noah and told him to build an ark. Noah had never seen an ark or a boat of any kind. Noah had actually never seen rain or any kind of flood. But God said, "Build an ark," and Noah began to build an ark. This construction project went on for many years, maybe up to one hundred years. Noah had no power tools, no heavy equipment, and very little help. The neighbors certainly were no help. The people around Noah were so wicked that God had decided to wipe the whole human race off the face of the earth except Noah, his wife, their three sons, and their wives. *Can you imagine how those evil neighbors must have tormented Noah through this long building project?* Rick thought. *They must have called out, "Noah, what are you doing?"*

"I'm building an ark."

"What's an ark?"

"A large boat."

"What's a boat?"

"A big wooden box that will float on the water."

"What water?"

"God is going to send rain."

"What's rain?"

You can fill in the rest of the blanks. It probably wasn't a pretty picture as those neighbors made Noah's life miserable year after year. Yet, in spite of all that, Noah kept acting on the basis of what God had commanded and promised. He was acting on promises concerning things he had never in his lifetime seen. You know, come to think of it, no one else had ever seen these things either. There was no historical record of the kind of thing God had said would happen.

The heroes of the faith that Rick remembered from all his Bible study, starting with Bible stories in Sunday school, were generally not real cautious people. They were people who wouldn't bow down in worship to the king even if it meant being thrown into a fiery furnace for this disobedience. Or a guy who wouldn't stop praying visibly even though it resulted in him being fed to lions as their midnight snack. They were men like David who walked up to a battle-hardened giant and proclaimed that he was going to chop off his head even though David's only weapon was a sling and some stones. There seemed to be a real disconnect between what he read in the Bible and what these men counseled. Rick began to wonder to himself, *What happened to the idea that we are to live "all out" for the Lord? Why do I see example after example in the Bible of people who trusted God to do things that were impossible from a human perspective, but these people today are afraid to take any risk?*

He remembered listening to a well-known preacher of a local mega-church whose service was broadcast on the radio.

That particular morning the preacher said to his congregation, "Thank you for braving the rain to come to the service this morning."

Rick began to wonder to himself, *What has the church come to when driving to church in our completely weather-tight cars on a Sunday morning when some rain is falling constitutes an act of bravery? Big risk there! Has the church gotten to the point that the bravest thing we do for the Lord, the biggest risk we take, is to drive to church on a rainy Sunday instead of staying home? Where did we get the idea that it is a godly thing to try to eliminate all risk from our lives?"*

Of course, there were plenty of the people in these churches who would run up their credit cards purchasing things like big screen HD TVs, iPads, and expensive vacations. Nothing seemed to be too big a risk in their personal lives when they wanted some new luxury or pleasure. The only risk they were afraid of was any risk regarding the Lord's work.

One of Rick's favorite verses was 2 Corinthians 5:7, "We live by faith, not by sight." There just was no way to define walking by faith without including risk. How could any congregation be pleasing to God if the people and leaders were completely unwilling to take any risk? In his office alone, Rick cried out, "How did we ever get this idea that the church should be free of all risk? What about the first century Christians who risked their lives every time they shared the gospel? Aren't they the model we're supposed to be following, not some cautious old coot who speaks against any decision that might require even a small amount of risk for the congregation?"

Rick was frustrated in the extreme as he tried to square what he read in the Bible with what he saw this church, and many others, practicing. He developed a chart he wanted to use the next time he preached in this congregation, although he knew he ran a risk himself if he did that. It was the risk of getting run out of town on a rail if he taught this. The chart was as follows:

WALKING BY SIGHT	WALKING BY FAITH
(The Comfort Zone)	(The Scary, Impossible Zone)
What we can do ourselves	Beyond what we can do ourselves
Our own resources are adequate	Our resources are not adequate
We have enough:	We don't have enough:
Strength	Strength
Wisdom	Wisdom
Money	Money
Power	Power
Clout	Clout

The chart shows that walking by faith means that we deliberately choose to live in the realm of that which is humanly impossible. It means we trust God to do things for which we do not have enough of our own human resources. We trust God to provide that for which we do not yet have enough money. We trust him to empower us when we don't have enough power for the task, such as being a witness. Rick often found himself saying to people, "It is very scary to live in this way for the very reason that we are attempting things that are humanly impossible. It isn't at all scary to walk by sight. We can depend on ourselves and whatever we already have enough of. But it is only in the faith zone, the humanly impossible zone, that we need God. If we continue to live in the walking by sight zone we feel safe, but that is such an illusion. When we live that way, we think we don't need the Lord to do anything beyond our own abilities. We forget that we need him every day to supply the air we breathe. He can bring our lives to an end at any moment. But we forget that and prefer to live in the illusion of our self-sufficiency."

Rick remembered how it used to frustrate him early in his ministry days when someone would say to him, "It just can't be done. It's impossible." But now he regarded that as almost a necessity before any course of action was taken. After all, if no one thought a plan was humanly impossible to complete, it wasn't walking by faith. Now when someone said to Rick that a thing was impossible he pumped his fist in the air and said, "Yes!" Now he knew that it meant he was walking by faith, not by sight. If only he could help churches to understand that they needed to act the same way.

He gradually began to notice church after church that was being stifled by their unwillingness to take any risk. *How can they expect God to do anything significant on their behalf if they are only willing to attempt that for which they don't need God anyway? No wonder the Lord isn't doing anything great on their behalf! They aren't expecting him to do anything beyond what they can do on their own. And they certainly are not willing to take any risk if it means depending on God to do anything for which they do not yet have the resources already in place.* He also began to remember that in the churches he had pastored they had taken great risks. They had attempted things so great that unless God intervened they were bound to fail.

When the churches he pastored had taken great risks God had intervened in great ways. He provided financially beyond anything they would have imagined. He provided resources of people who were eager to serve in just the right places. And he provided contacts with people who needed to know the Lord and were open to the gospel message. Maybe there was a principle there. God acts when we expect him to. God acts when we trust him to act. And God acts when we trust him for that which is humanly impossible and step off the banks of the Jordan River into the water before God parts it.

Now if he could only get more churches to understand that this was one of the foremost principles of church growth. If they wanted God to use them significantly to reach people who had not yet decided to trust in Jesus, they would have to step out in faith into the scary, impossible zone of what they could not do with their own resources. He had always practiced this as a pastor, but now he had to find a way to get churches that had been living in a very different way to embrace this thoroughly biblical principle. How could he do that? He was going to have to talk this over with his two compatriots in this struggle to awaken churches.

QUESTIONS FOR REFLECTION

1. Define "walking by faith."
2. What happens when we "walk by sight"?

DO MY BIDDING

WHAT'S WRONG AT OAK CREEK COMMUNITY CHURCH? Wayne wondered. *They have every reason to be a dynamic, growing congregation. They have great Bible teaching from their pastor, a great facility, one of the best staffs he had ever seen in a church, a great children's ministry, a great youth program, and a worship band to die for. But the congregation has been at a plateau for years and is now beginning to decline. The senior pastor, Jack, has that look in his eyes that says he is about to give up, not just on this church but on the ministry as a whole. It seems that other occupations are starting to look pretty attractive to this effective man of God. Of course, he might get his wish sooner rather than later. This church has a reputation for getting a new pastor every five to seven years no matter how well the current pastor has done his job.* Wayne wondered, *What is that all about?*

He scheduled a meeting with the senior pastor. At the meeting Wayne reassured Jack that nothing he said would be used against him in any way. He just wanted to try to get some perspective on why this church continued to fail in its mandate to reach lost people with the gospel in significant numbers and grow. Once Jack was reassured that he was not going to pay a price for being open about things, he began to open up.

"It all started," he said, "within the first week of my tenure at Oak Creek. One of the long-time members had casually dropped the comment in conversation that 'pastors come and pastors go, but the church remains.'" Jack had not responded to that comment, but he had been stung by it. The more he thought about it the madder he got. This man was saying to him, "Well, sonny, you will be here for a little while, and then you will leave. Your being here really won't make any difference because 'we' are in charge around here." Jack understood that the "we" was the lay people of the church.

It was even more evident when he looked over the new by-laws that the church had adopted prior to his arrival as pastor. The by-laws spent a great many words on explaining the roles and importance of the lay leaders, but almost no words on the role and importance of the pastor. In fact, the actual language was quite amazing. It said something to the effect of, "Since it seems prudent to have a pastor, here is how we will go about selecting one." It gave no detail as to what his role was to be. In fact, it spent much more time on explaining how the church could go about getting rid of the pastor when they decided to do that. It was almost as though the by-laws regarded the pastor as a necessary evil to be tolerated as long as he did not disrupt the real power base of the church.

That was just the beginning of a downward slide. The elders of the church made it very clear to Jack over the next few months that they were in charge of the church. They let him know loud and clear that they were his bosses, and he was their employee. As long as he did nothing to ruffle their feathers, as long as he held them up before the church as the real leaders of the church, and as long as he gave them clear indications that he accepted this arrangement he would be allowed to continue to teach on Sunday mornings. But if he tried to initiate any new direction for the church, if he tried to be the leader of the church, if he did anything that appeared to threaten their position of power—their stranglehold on the church—he was as good as gone. Jack had proven in his previous church that he was a gifted leader who could lead the church to great effectiveness in reaching out to un-churched people. If he was allowed to lead, the church would begin to grow very significantly. But he was not being allowed to lead, and it appeared that would be the case for the foreseeable future. Wayne could clearly understand why Jack was about ready to hang up his cleats and call it a day. Jack was frustrated out of his gourd!

This really concerned Wayne. *What's a regional superintendent to do in a case like this?* he wondered. One thing was very clear to him. The way this church was conducting itself was absolutely not what was taught in Scripture. Over and over again in the Bible he saw examples of the fact that when God wanted something done, he always started by raising up one individual. God never raised up a committee. He called one person, implanted the vision in that person, who then passed that vision to others who caught the vision and joined the cause. That one person didn't operate as a law unto himself, but he was clearly the leader that God had appointed. Wayne also realized that this was the case in all the great things the Lord was doing in our day as well. Every dynamically growing church had a pastor who was clearly the leader of the church. Every para-church movement had begun when God placed the vision in the heart of one person who then spread the vision to others who joined in the cause. He looked at examples such as Bill Bright, Billy Graham, Rick Warren, James Dobson, and Bill Hybels.

Maybe I should change my name to Bill! he thought. But, on a more serious note, he knew that Oak Creek Church and many more like it had a serious problem, a problem of misunderstanding who was to lead. In almost every church in his care, there was at least some measure of tension over this question of who was to lead. The more he thought about it the more he realized that there are two profoundly important questions that every church and every Christian must answer. The right answers would result in a healthy, growing congregation. The wrong answer would result in a stunted church and miserable Christians.

The two questions were: 1) Why does this church exist? and 2) Who is in charge here? He could clearly see that in the case of Trinity Church the typical answer given by Christians with regard to why the church exists is "to serve me, to make me happy, to devote itself to satisfying my every 'need.'" He also could see that the biblical answer was that the church exists to serve God and do his will, the most important part of which is to reach lost people with the gospel and lead all Christians to become obedient and faithful disciples of Jesus Christ. With regard to the second question, several answers were given. In some churches the answer to "Who's in charge here?" was "We are all in charge. This is a democracy." That was especially true in his denomination, which historically had been strongly congregational in their style of government. In other churches there was a tendency to say, "The elders are in charge." But in almost none of his churches would the people have answered that the pastor was in charge.

Those answers did not seem to be in agreement with what he read in Scripture and saw lived out in how God worked in churches and para-church organizations in our day.

The people of the churches and their duly elected officials resisted pastoral leadership because they wanted to be in charge. They wanted to control the church. They wanted to control the decisions that it made. Why was this so important to them? Well, it was starting to look suspiciously like it came from a desire to make sure the church did what they wanted it to do. They wanted to control the outcome so their "needs" would be met. But the pastor, in most cases, had a different agenda.

Oh, yeah, Wayne remembered. *There are so many people in these churches who use their position of service or leadership to gain self-esteem. Those people will do anything to protect their turf, to make sure that they are able to continue being a big fish in a small pond.* Of course that attitude made it particularly difficult for the pastor to lead. He couldn't change anything, no matter how bad the condition of the church, because any change would threaten someone's little personal kingdom.

Wayne saw so clearly that the real needs of these people were not to be entertained, pampered, coddled, and made to feel important. What they actually needed was to be trained how to live lives of service and obedience to the Lord as John 14:21 and 23, and John 15:10-11 tell us:

> "Whoever has my commands and obeys them, he is the one who loves me. He who loves me will be loved by my Father, and I too will love him and show myself to him"…Jesus replied, "If anyone loves me, he will obey my teaching. My Father will love him, and we will come to him and make our home with him…If you obey my commands you will remain in my love, just as I have obeyed my Father's commands and remain in his love. I

have told you this so that my joy may be in you and that your joy may be complete."

Wayne frequently reminded people from these verses that it is only in obeying the Lord's commands and trusting his promises that we find real joy, complete joy. The most central command he has given the church in our day is to make disciples of as many people as we possibly can. If we disobey the Lord in his last command to the church, how can we possibly find the joy the Lord has in mind for us? When whole churches, indeed, the church as a whole in America, is disobedient to the command to spread the gospel with power, and at great risk to ourselves, we will have a whole lot of miserable churches and many individual Christians who are frustrated.

He had seen so often that when the focus of the churches changes from outreach to "meeting our own needs," people in the churches start becoming very selfish. They want everything to be oriented to their wishes. And they don't want any pastor suggesting that the church exists for a reason higher than their own selfish desires. When Win Arn did his research decades ago and found that 89 percent of the Christians in that day believed that the church existed "to take care of them and their families", he also found that 91 percent of the pastors believed that the church exists primarily to reach lost people. Wayne had seen the tension this sets up in churches. Most of the people in the churches believe that the pastor is supposed to devote himself to taking care of them while most of the pastors believe the church's main focus is to be on reaching lost people. No wonder people don't want to follow the leadership of their pastor! He is urging them to devote themselves to the cause of reaching lost people while all they want is for him to devote himself to coddling them. Wayne knew that unless pastors are allowed to exercise their God-ordained leadership, churches are doomed to continue to decline. Pastors are raised up by the Lord not to make people comfortable. They are raised up to lead people to risk all in the only cause worth giving our lives to, the cause of reaching as many people with the gospel as we possibly can.

Wayne knew that it takes a pastor with real courage to buck the prevailing opinion of the church members and say, "My primary purpose is not serving you. It is training you to serve the Lord and obey his command to make disciples of as many people as we can." Not surprisingly, many pastors just play it safe and go along with the demands of the church members. When that happens, the whole church becomes disobedient to the Lord. The pastor is called to lead the church into obedience and to train them to be effective servants, not just serve them.

QUESTIONS FOR REFLECTION

1. Is it clear who is leading your church?
2. Does your pastor have the required freedom to lead your church?

WEEK ONE
STUDY GUIDE

1. Brainstorm, with the leader writing your answers on a whiteboard or large sheet of paper: What do you believe are the main reasons for the decline of the church in America?

2. Take five minutes and have each person in the group draw a rough sketch representing what they see as the current condition of their church (the organization, not the building). Have each person share *briefly* with the group what their drawing communicates.

3. Break into groups of three or four people and answer the question: What evidences of a "consumer mentality" are there in our church? Then report back to the whole group what you concluded.

4. Discuss as a whole group: Why is there such a struggle over who is to lead the church?

5. Have the individual members of the group take five minutes to answer this question: According to the chapter "Do My Bidding," what is the biblical pattern for leadership? Then report their findings back to the group.

WEEK TWO

TEACH ME BIBLE FACTS

WHEN WAYNE, AL, AND RICK GOT TOGETHER OR TALKED ON THE PHONE, THEY ALSO SHARED CONCERNS FROM THEIR PERSONAL LIVES. Rick's wife, Marilyn, was scheduled to have serious spinal surgery, and Al's nineteen-year-old son, Matt, really seemed to be wandering through life at this point. He had begun to question what he believed. Al realized that many young people go through a stage in which they need to discover their faith for themselves. It is just too easy to accept beliefs from one's parents without examining those premises for oneself, and then choose to believe in them, independent of one's parents' beliefs. But it was especially hard for ministry parents to watch this process and allow their children to go through it for themselves. These three amigos prayed for each other as they shared these concerns. But it seemed they inevitably came back to talking about the churches in their regions.

Grace Church was especially troubling to them. It was clear to them what the problem was. But how could they get the people of this church, especially their pastor, to face the reality of what was really happening? How could they make them see that their approach was the reason the church was in decline?

Grace Church was very proud of their acumen in "rightly dividing the Scriptures." Their pastor had graduated ten years before from a seminary that really emphasized the teaching role of the pastor. While it may not have been directly articulated by all the professors, the message was very clear. The primary role of the pastor was to teach the scriptures. It was even said by some of them, "Just teach the word and everything else will fall in place." These three superintendents understood that teaching the Word accurately was essential to the health of the church, but they also realized that it was not the very most important role for the pastor. The pastor leading the church was every bit as important as his teaching the word accurately. All three of these men had often wondered why, at ordination councils, the whole emphasis had been on questioning the candidate for ordination's doctrinal orthodoxy. No one had asked any questions about whether this person, on whom they were about to confer the authority to pastor a church, had exhibited any leadership gifts and skills at all. Clearly this just wasn't that important to the people who made up the ordination council. That really bothered Rick, Wayne, and Al. They understood only too well that, while doctrinal orthodoxy was critically important, there was something that was being overlooked. The men who were failing to be good pastors in their region were not failing because of not being doctrinally correct. They were failing because of being poor leaders. But that factor was not even being examined in ordination councils throughout their regions. To make matters worse, the pastor at Grace Church had been thoroughly ingrained with the idea that there was really only one style of preaching that was acceptable to God. In this view, only verse-by-verse, expository preaching of the Word was acceptable to God. Topical preaching was regarded as anathema by this crowd. They thought God would never bless any preaching other than expository.

Rick, Wayne, and Al had all received a great deal of this philosophy when they were in seminary themselves, but it surprised them that when they read the Scriptures they couldn't find any examples of expository preaching in the Bible. They could find plenty of examples of topical preaching but no exegetical sermons in the Bible. Surely if God had intended that this be the only acceptable form of preaching for his people, he would have included some examples of this form of teaching in his Word. There came to be a sort of intellectual elitism that characterized churches with this powerful commitment to only this one form of preaching. These churches came to look a whole lot more like a seminary classroom than like a group of people mobilized to storm the gates of hell and set Satan's captives free. Even some churches that included some topical preaching in their schedule seemed so committed to an academic model of the church that it was stifling the growth of the church.

The pastors and some of the people in these churches seemed to think that the highest purpose of the church was the transfer of Bible facts from the gray matter of the preacher to the gray matter of the people. It was assumed that if the people of the church just learned more Bible facts, then the church would be a church that was pleasing to God. No one seemed to ask, "What are people supposed to do with all this factual content once they have absorbed it?" In these churches it was almost as though the people were packing in Bible facts to pass some final exam so they would get their degree. The problem was that no one seemed to ever do much with these facts once they were accumulated. Actually, they did do one thing. They became proud of their Bible knowledge! The Bible warns us of this in 1 Corinthians 8:1 when it warns us that, "Knowledge puffs up, but love builds up." For these people it was almost as though they were in some junior high bible quiz competition. The race was on to see who could accumulate the most Bible knowledge, and they competed with each other. The one with the most knowledge was assumed to be the most spiritual.

But, these superintendents thought, *that isn't what we find in the Bible. In the Bible we find that the one who is most obedient to the Word is the one who is most spiritual. It really doesn't matter how much you know if you are not obeying the commands you know and trusting in the promises you know.*

Sometimes it seemed that some of these churches had degenerated to nothing more than stations for cognitive transfer. People came, sat, listened, took notes, and then didn't do anything with what they had learned. What good did it do for the preacher to just keep spewing out Bible facts if the people did not begin to live out what they were taught? At times when he was still a pastor, Rick grew so frustrated with teaching people who did nothing with what the Word taught that he used to tease his people by saying that he was going to teach this biblical principle this week. The next week he would check to see how many people were living according to it. If only 50 percent were living by it, he would preach the same message over again that week. The week after, he would check again to see how many were now living according to what had been taught. Until at least 90 percent were living according to the commands and promises of that passage of scripture, he would just keep teaching that same message over and over again. He had never had the courage to actually do that, but by saying it a few times people actually understood what he was getting at.

They had seen that in the academic model church, no one, from the pastor on down, seems to pay any attention to whether the Word is making any difference in people's lives. It is just assumed that by teaching the facts the preacher has done his job. Why, just that morning, Rick had heard one of the leading proponents of the church as a classroom speaking on the radio. He had said, "The purpose of the pastor is to teach the Word." Of course the pastor is to teach the Word, but that isn't all he is supposed to do. This famous preacher on the radio made it sound like that was the whole or main purpose of the pastor with everything else coming in a distant second or third.

But, thought Rick, *what about all the places in the Bible where the preacher is told to reprove, rebuke, and exhort his people? That isn't just teaching the facts. It is urging the people to live according to commands and promises we find in the Scriptures. The definition of the word* rebuke *is "to criticize or reprove sharply, to reprimand." That goes way beyond just teaching the facts. It implies holding people accountable to obey the commands and trust in the promises of the Word. In the academic model church there is little of this accountability. It is assumed that if we just teach the Word that is all we need to do. In these churches there is very little measuring of any measurable accomplishments like how many people accepted Christ this year. In their view it is enough to accurately teach the Word and assume that everything else is going to just happen naturally, with no effort being made to insure that it happens.*

The superintendents knew that, in reality, the church was to be viewed much more like a training center. They saw that to make disciples required that churches both teach and train people. The Great Commission in Matthew 28:18-20 commands us to "make disciples of all the nations… teaching them *to obey* everything that I have commanded you." They knew that it wasn't enough to just teach people what Jesus taught. We also have to teach them to obey what Jesus taught and what the rest of the Word teaches. The academic model church stops with just teaching the facts. Consequently, people don't become mature. They become knowledgeable, but that is not the same thing as mature. Maturity requires that the people begin to live out the truths of the Bible in their lives on a consistent basis.

They were only too aware that once we accept Christ as our Savior we enter into spiritual warfare. God calls us to begin to live for him, including spreading the gospel with great passion and effectiveness so that many more people come to faith in Jesus. Satan fights back against that commitment with everything he can muster. To be able to win in warfare requires a great deal of training. It involves some classroom-type teaching in which there is the presentation of the factual content that is necessary. But it doesn't stop there. It moves out of the classroom into training in the activities of warfare. In military training the pilots start with little gliders, then move up to small, single-engine training planes, and eventually they are flying fighter jets, bombers, and huge jumbo transport planes. They fly those planes in simulated combat conditions to be prepared for the real battles to come. If all they did was sit in the classroom receiving the transfer of factual knowledge to their brains, they would get those same brains blown out as soon as they were in a real combat situation. There is only so much that can be learned in a classroom environment. But tragically, some of the churches they were responsible for amounted to not much more than one giant classroom. The "professor" dumped his cognitive load of facts on the people once, twice, or even three times a week, but that is as far as it ever went. They were never trained to win the battle that is occurring in the real world.

Rick knew that as long as the leaders of these churches continued to live in this fantasy land of believing that it was all about teaching facts, these churches would continue to decline. He knew that no one's life is transformed by just the transfer of factual information. Lives are transformed when the factual information is then translated into action in a person's real life situation. He was concerned that these churches absolutely must begin to insist on obedience to what is taught, not just learning the facts. The style of preaching is far less important than the outcome of that same preaching. If the truths of God's Word are taught in such a way that people are urged to live out those truths and begin to actually do so, it really doesn't matter whether the truth is delivered in an expository or a topical style. But if Bible facts are taught and people are not urged and held accountable to live those truths, it likewise really doesn't matter whether the truth is delivered in an expository or a topical style. There will be no transformation taking place in people's lives. Rick kept urging pastors to see that teaching people to obey goes far beyond just teaching the facts. It involves exhorting, reproving, and rebuking people; urging them to get busy doing what the Bible commands; and correcting them when they fail to do so. It involves creating "practice" situations so that the people of the church have the opportunity to begin to live out the activities of serving the Lord while under guidance and supervision. It requires holding people accountable to living according to the commands and promises of the Word. There is far too little of that occurring in our churches, but especially in the academic model churches.

Rick remembered that when he had been a pastor himself, some of the people in the church seemed to regard it as an oddity that he had such a passion for reaching lost people. They used to say things to him like, "You should be an evangelist," or "Maybe you will be the next Billy Graham." What Rick found so disturbing about this is that these people regarded a pastor who had a passion for reaching lost people as not being in the proper role. It was almost as if they were saying, "Well, this isn't right. Pastors are not supposed to be so committed to reaching lost people. Their job is to take care of us and teach us." They regarded a pastor with a passion for reaching lost people as abnormal. Rick believed that the pastor who doesn't have such a passion should be regarded as abnormal! What a sad commentary on the state of the church in America that when a pastor has a deep desire for the church to be effective in reaching lost people he is regarded as an anomaly who should really be doing something other than being a pastor.

The superintendents began to wonder, *What can we do to inspire churches to begin to produce disciples who are actually obeying the commands of God and trusting in his promises? Somehow we have to get them out of the thinking that it is enough just to convey biblical content to people's brains. How can we inspire the leaders of churches to make the transformation of people's lives the goal of the church, not just teaching them Bible facts that they do nothing with?*

This really began to weigh on these men's hearts. They knew this wasn't just an academic question. The very life of these churches depended on finding an answer to this dilemma.

QUESTIONS FOR REFLECTION

1. Does your church show any signs of being an academic model church?
2. What causes this type of church to be ineffective in reaching unchurched people?

LET'S HAVE FUN

WHENEVER WAYNE FELT THE URGE FOR SOME GOOD OLD CHURCH POTLUCK FOOD HE AND HIS WIFE, CHLOE, KNEW EXACTLY WHERE TO HEAD. Fellowship Church certainly lived up to its name. They really had fun together. If they would have been honest about it, they should have stated that their church's mission was to have a good time with their Christian friends. When you examined their list of volunteer leaders there were sure a lot with titles that, while usually given a slightly more spiritual sounding name, really should have been called party coordinators. Their annual budget reflected a heavy emphasis on "fellowship events." Every time they got together there had better be coffee and some kind of goodies or people would begin to grumble! And it was a fun church to pastor. Except when the pastor looked at the attendance numbers for the past year as he prepared his annual report it wasn't so much fun. Inevitably the numbers were down. Year after year the same story prevailed. The pastor wondered how that could be since it was such a friendly, happy church. They had women's brunches, softball leagues, men's breakfasts, Dinners for Six programs, adult Sunday school classes that were so entertaining, fall parties, Christmas banquets, and many more such events. Why would anyone not want to be part of such a fun bunch? But for some reason people were staying away in droves.

Wayne attended there for a few Sundays to try to get a grasp on what was happening. Or maybe it was a matter of what wasn't happening there. The first thing he noticed was the preponderance of "donkey circles" in the foyer. He knew that when wild donkeys were threatened by a predator, they gathered in a circle with their heads in the center and their powerfully kicking hind legs out toward the predator. Woe to the mountain lion that tried to get past that brutal barrier! He saw the same arrangement in the church foyer. Groups of six or eight church members were clustered together with their faces in the center of the circle and their behinds out. If a newcomer walked into the foyer, these Christian donkeys would occasionally look over their shoulder for a second and turn back to their group. The impression that was given was, "Just try to get into this group! We will kick you off!" None of these people would have admitted that they had any such thoughts in their heads. But the reality was that they were just too busy hanging out with the friends they already had to allow anyone else into their circle. They called it "fellowship."

But when Wayne looked at the Bible, he saw a different definition of fellowship.

It goes beyond just having fun with our Christian friends, he thought. *It speaks of fellowship with Jesus. It seems unlikely that fellowship with Jesus revolves around coffee and donuts. It also speaks of the fellowship of suffering. That doesn't exactly sound like having fun. And fellowship with the Holy Spirit probably doesn't involve a church potluck. Clearly when the Bible talks about fellowship, it means a whole lot more than just food and fun with our Christian friends. There seems to be something much more substantial about it than just pleasure.*

Wayne got the impression that it involved commitment to one another, holding one another accountable, sacrificing for one another, sharing the deep feelings and issues of one's life. Again, it sounds a whole lot more like what one experiences in warfare. That sure made more sense when he considered that we really are in war. Biblical fellowship sounds a lot more like what men experience in a foxhole while fully engaged in combat. It involves praying for each other, sharing the truths of Scriptures—not just as an intellectual curiosity but as the very bread of life. It involves protecting each other from the attacks of the enemy, which sometimes means rebuking each other when one strayed into the path of Satan's arrows. It means consoling one another when one suffers a loss and rejoicing together when one experiences a victory. But most of all it means committing ourselves together to the goal of victory. In the church a big part of victory is seeing significant numbers of people coming to faith in Jesus Christ. When he really looked at it, what Fellowship Church was experiencing was really not biblical fellowship at all. It was just having fun with their friends and putting a spiritual justification on their own pleasure seeking.

But that wasn't the worst thing about it. The worst part was that all that emphasis on what they called fellowship was preventing them from reaching out to other people. They thought, *Surely people would want to join a group that has so much fun together!* But the problem was that the only people having the fun were the people who were already in the group. For people who came to visit the church, it was anything but fun. They felt like outsiders from the moment they walked in the front door. What felt like a close-knit group to the people who were already part of it felt like an impenetrable clique to anyone who was new to the church. Not only were they confronted with all those donkey circles in the foyer, but the service was full of inside jokes, which just served to reinforce that they didn't belong. And clearly the people in the church didn't really have any time for them. They might give them a real friendly handshake and say, "I'm so glad that you visited today." But then they hurried off to find their friends. They couldn't miss out on any of the latest gossip! Who knows? Someone might even issue an invitation to a backyard barbecue that they might miss if they were hanging around with this new person for very long.

Wayne saw that what it came down to was something very simple. It was just another way in which the Christians who were already part of the church were being very selfish. They had not made it a priority to reach out to people who were not yet part of the group. Their real priority was their own commitment to fun with each other. Real fellowship was based on the fact that the participants are fully engaged in the warfare of battering down the gates of hell and setting Satan's captives free. But that wasn't what the folks at Fellowship Church were all about. Oh, they spiritualized their commitment to what they called "fellowship." They said that it was what they needed to make them strong Christians. But the question was, "Strong for what?" If they had no commitment to obedience to the Great Commission to make disciples of as many people as they possibly could, what did they need to be strong for? Was it just that they needed to be strong in order to keep their lives all safe and secure, all cozy with one another, to protect their children against any possible negative influence in their lives, and to eliminate all risk in their lives? Did they need to be strong just so that they could face the inevitable trials of life like a flat tire or the TV breaking down or their child throwing a temper tantrum or the doctor's report that their cholesterol was too high from all that partying?

Wayne knew that Satan's strategies are usually very subtle. If he can get us to substitute something that, in itself, seems quite harmless in place of the battle to free souls from his clutches, he rejoices. Satan knows that if a church has a high commitment to what they call "fellowship," which is really just fun with their friends, they are harmless to him. They will never threaten his grasp on a large part of the population. He loves it when churches get all wrapped up in what seems like such a harmless thing. He really loves it when they spiritualize it to the point that they actually think that they are doing the will of God when, in reality, they are just indulging their desire for fun.

Wayne knew that real fellowship could not be experienced outside of the battlefield environment. Only when we commit ourselves to victory over Satan will we know the kind of bonding together that we so long for. He thought, *How tragic that so many people are willing to accept this cheap substitute for what they really long for. There really is very little genuine fellowship occurring in the churches in America because so few are committed to reaching lost people. If indeed only 4 percent of the population is currently making decisions to trust in Jesus as their Savior, it isn't that the gospel has less power in our day. It is that we are not proclaiming the gospel with zeal, enthusiasm, and with any risk to ourselves. In the absence of this core obedience to the command of Jesus to make disciples, there will be very little genuine fellowship.*

He grieved that there is another tragedy with indulging in this cheap substitute for genuine fellowship. It never satisfies. It always leaves the participants empty. Wayne was only too aware that it is only as we commit ourselves to obedience to the Lord that we experience fullness of joy. It frustrated him to no end that so many of the people in the churches he oversaw were willing, even eager, to settle for a cheap substitute for the real thing. Had no one ever really taught them the truth of Matthew 16:25, "For whoever wants to save his life will lose it, but whoever loses his life for me will find it"? He had often said to people individually and in preaching, "Pursuing fellowship for the sake of fellowship will result in emptiness. Fellowship is the result of the commitment to be in the trenches fighting the battle against Satan and his forces. In those trenches a bonding occurs that cannot take place anywhere else. It is the result of a commitment to lose one's life for his sake. When we make that commitment we find life, but it is a different kind of life. It is a life of peace and contentment in the Lord. That doesn't mean a life with only peaceable circumstances. Quite often this life has its share of tumult and trial. How can one be in war and not experience hardship? But it means that in the middle of battle, there is a peace that can only come from the Lord. Real fellowship rejoices in the supernatural peace that God gives people who are wholly committed to doing his will."

Another problem Wayne saw with the pseudo fellowship is that it is based on selfishness that inevitably leads to petty little squabbles as each person is trying to stake out their own turf and protect their own interests. When they were living a life of selfishness they ended up behaving like selfish little children. If someone horned in on their party or "stole" one of their friends or said something that they regarded as an insult, they responded like a child. They fought back or bickered or took their ball and went home. When people engaged in pseudo fellowship they ended up messing up the fun they were trying to have. People who were behaving selfishly toward the Lord and his will for their lives always ended up behaving selfishly toward each other. Under the surface of all the seeming fun of a fellowship church were hurts, animosities, bickering, jealousy, and outright hatred toward other people. The fellowship was just an illusion. How much better to lose one's life for his sake and find the much better life that comes from living all out for him? When people lived like that they were able to enjoy the real fellowship that comes from being in the trenches together, from fighting their real enemy shoulder to shoulder.

QUESTIONS FOR REFLECTION

1. How might "fellowship" hinder us from reaching un-churched people for Christ?

2. What are the characteristics of true fellowship?

STIR MY EMOTIONS

RICK'S WIFE, MARILYN, HAD COME SAFELY THROUGH THE SURGERY ON HER BACK AND WAS DOING PRETTY WELL. She was walking around quite a bit, had minimal pain, and her appetite had returned, so Rick was feeling relieved about that. He had experienced the usual pre-surgery jitters anticipating the things that could go wrong in her surgery experience. But it had turned out as well as any surgery could, and he was grateful for her return to much better health. She was really doing considerably better than she had been before the surgery. Now his mind began to turn back to his concerns for the churches.

Celebration Church had gone through some changes in the last five years that were beginning to concern him. They had, historically, been a pretty bland church. Nothing unusual there, just the usual church service, Sunday school, youth ministry, and choir. But recently, they had begun to place a great deal of emphasis on the worship experience of the people. It had been quite a change for this usually staid church. They had developed a terrific worship band. Their worship leader was doing a fine job, and the people were really starting to get into the worship experience. They sang with such passion, raised their hands, were even beginning to sort of dance around as they stood in front of their seats. Clearly this was becoming a much more emotional experience. The people were actually enjoying the worship experience, whereas before they had just kind of sleep walked through that part of the service.

So what's the problem? Rick thought. *Who could find anything wrong with that? I must be becoming paranoid, or am I just so much of an old stuck-in-the-mud kind of guy that I can't adapt to this new reality in worship?*

But no, there was something more that was concerning Rick about this.

As he thought about it, Rick began to wonder who they were really worshiping. It wasn't that there was anything wrong with this style of worship. In fact there were many things right about it. Enthusiasm in worship and active participation in worship were certainly good things. Their worship was definitely relevant to the cultural style of the un-churched people around them, and that was a powerfully important thing. But were they worshiping God or were they worshiping worship? Were they just finding the emotional satisfaction from this type of worship service so pleasing that it had become an end in itself? Over the years Rick had wrestled inside himself to find an accurate definition of worship. He had concluded that worship starts with a recognition of who God is and what he has done. That information comes primarily from what God has revealed to us in his Word, not first from our experience. Then, there is a proper response to the recognition of who God is and what he has done in the world and on our behalf. The proper response includes awe, praise, trust, peace, contentment, and obedience. Ah, there is that word again! Real worship must include obedience, as Saul found out 1 Samuel 15. God had commanded him to utterly destroy the Amalekites and all of their possessions. But Saul and his men had kept some of the spoil for themselves, including the best sheep. When Saul and his men were confronted by the prophet Samuel, the prophet asked why they had not obeyed the Lord. Saul replied that they had obeyed, but Samuel said, "Oh yeah, then what's with the bleating of the sheep I hear?" He went on to rebuke Saul severely with these words, "Does the Lord delight in burnt offerings and sacrifices as much as in obeying the voice of the Lord? To obey is better than sacrifice, and to heed is better than the fat of rams." All the sacrifices in the world could not make up for the disobedience of Saul and his men.

Rick began to realize that, in so many of the churches, people were getting into the act of worship while living in gross disobedience to the clear command of the Lord. How were they disobedient? No one had come to faith in Jesus through his or her efforts in the last six months. In fact, if Rick looked at the last six years, most of these churches had seen almost no conversions of anyone other than their own children, and even those were becoming increasingly rare. Clearly they were disobedient to the last command of Jesus to make disciples of as many people as they possibly could in the shortest time possible. They were living in blatant disobedience to the Lord on an on-going basis. If they were in disobedience, was this really worship of God that they were experiencing? It is impossible to be simultaneously worshiping God and disobeying him. At Celebration Church many people were having a wonderful emotional experience during the worship service. It felt so good to sing with such abandon. The newfound freedom to raise their hands and dance around a little bit felt wonderful. For those with a feelings-oriented personality all this felt like a little bit of heaven. It was like they were finally coming home. But the problem was that it wasn't really worship. It would only have been worship if they had been living in obedience to the Lord.

Rick taught people that, "Worship is supposed to bring glory to God. In John 15:8 Jesus said, 'This is to my Father's glory, that you bear much fruit, showing yourselves to be my disciples.' Certainly, there are several parts to what makes up 'fruit,' but one of the most important parts is people won to faith in Christ. Fruit includes things like the fruit of the Holy Spirit, but that isn't all fruit is. The results of effective evangelism are a very important part of fruit. God is glorified when many people come to trust in Jesus as their Savior. The absence of that kind of fruit means there are many less people bringing praise to God in worship. We cannot say we are worshiping God if our lives and our church do not result in significant numbers of people placing their faith in Jesus for the forgiveness of their sins and as the Lord of their lives."

Well, if it wasn't worship then what was it? Rick wondered. The more he thought about it, the more Rick realized that it came back to that old bugaboo called selfishness. This was people getting something for themselves. They were getting an emotional high, a wonderful experience. But it really wasn't focused on God. It was focused on themselves. In fact, for many of these people worship had become an end in itself. The high point of their Sunday morning was the good feeling they got from the experience of what they called worship. In genuine worship there is only one audience. Rick had come to believe that most people in church think of themselves as the audience, with the people up front being the performers. False! In worship, the only audience is God. The people up front are the prompters. And all the people in the seats are the performers. They are all to be performing worship to God. Now it seemed like this new worship style at Celebration Church certainly fit that bill since the people in the seats really seemed to be getting into the worship experience a whole lot more. But the big problem with this went right back to what Saul had done. He had gone through the motions of worship in the hopes of getting something for himself—the approval of God—but those motions took place when he was in the midst of full-blown disobedience to the Lord. These people were doing worship because they got something out of it for themselves. They got to feel good emotionally for forty-five minutes every Sunday, but they also were in the midst of full-blown disobedience to the Lord in the matter of reaching lost people with the gospel.

Rick was starting to realize that there were so many things that could be used as a substitute for obedience to God in the core issue of spreading the gospel to many people. He saw that we human beings are very adept at finding something, anything, to do, rather than the hard work of doing evangelism. But only effective evangelism will see to it that the church even exists after this generation passes away, as inevitably it will. Only effective evangelism fulfills the greatest reason the Lord left the church in the world. He left us here to free as many people from the bondage of Satan as we possibly can. We are to actively and aggressively storm the gates of hell, batter them down, and set people free who are in bondage to the world, the flesh, and the devil. Anything short of doing this successfully is a failure to be obedient to the Lord. We can accept no excuses for not doing this, and we can accept no substitutes for success in doing this. Anything less is disobedience and failure. Rick was becoming passionately aware that it was time to get rid of the excuses and substitutes and start experiencing the real thing.

He knew that enthusiastic worship in which the people of the church really get into the experience of worship is a great thing, but it is only worship if it is in the context of obedience to the Lord in the core command of the New Testament. We are instructed in Romans 12:1, "Therefore, I urge you, brothers, in view of God's mercy, to offer your bodies as living sacrifices, holy and pleasing to God—this is your spiritual act of worship." He wanted to cry out to people, "It is worship to present our bodies, our whole beings, as a sacrifice. That doesn't mean we are to set our bodies on fire as a sacrifice. It means we commit everything we are to the Lord in obedient service. We don't hold anything back! We trust every promise he has given to us enough that we take action based on that promise. And we obey every command he has given us without making any excuses, without rationalizing, and without trying to find any way out of this obedience. When we live this way our whole life is an act of service. When we live this way our corporate worship on Sunday morning or Saturday evening or whenever we get together to worship will be genuine and true worship. Then it will be really exciting to participate in worship with great enthusiasm. It will also mean that there will be a whole lot more new believers worshiping with us." In fact, Rick began to imagine how wonderful that worship would be when there were a bunch of new Christians coming to participate in worship with them on a regular basis.

Rick found himself longing for the day when each of his churches was known for exciting worship, not just Celebration Church. And this would be worship not just as a means of getting an emotional high for those participating. It would be true worship based on obedience to the commands of God. It would be true worship based on trusting the promises of God enough to take action in keeping with what the Lord had promised. Those promises include Acts 1:8, "You will receive power when the Holy Spirit comes upon you and you will be my witnesses in Jerusalem, Judea, Samaria, and to the uttermost parts of the earth," and Matthew 28:18-20, "All authority in heaven and on earth has been given to me. Therefore go and make disciples of all the nations…And Lo, I am with you always even to the end of the age."

Now that would be worship! Please bring this to pass, Lord, Rick prayed.

QUESTIONS FOR REFLECTION

1. How are you feeling about the worship services in your church?

2. Are you directing your worship to God when you attend the Sunday service at your church?

LET'S BE HOLIER

DIVISION STREET CHURCH CONCERNED AL MAYBE MORE THAN ALL THE OTHER CHURCHES IN HIS REGION. It had no hope of reaching any significant number of unbelievers if it continued on its current path. At first glance it seemed like what they were doing was a good thing. They had become very committed lately to the pursuit of holiness.

Now, what could be wrong with that? thought Al.

But the problem was they were not chasing after real holiness. They were accepting a substitute for the real thing. Al found it interesting how often Satan's best work comes in getting us to accept something that only seems to be the real thing. He is the master of disguise. He even disguises himself as an angel of light! The people Al knew seemed especially prone to accept a cheap imitation of genuine holiness. That cheap imitation usually came in the form of some kind of legalism. It involved some kind of rule making that goes beyond the Scriptures and made a matter of some person's preference into a rule that all were expected to follow with no variations.

At Division Street Church it showed up with regard to several concerns. The first was with regard to home schooling. Home schooling is a fine alternative for some families. Al personally knew of several very brilliant people who had gotten the first eight or twelve years of their education at home. It had served them extremely well. The problem at Division Church is that home schooling came to be regarded not just as one good alternative. It came to be seen as a measure of a family's spirituality. In their view, if you weren't home schooling your children, you were really an unspiritual family. It didn't matter if neither parent had the least amount of ability and interest in home schooling. It didn't matter if the parents' work schedule made home schooling virtually impossible. It didn't matter if your children were going to a fine Christian school. It didn't matter if your children were thriving in the public school, maintaining a close walk with the Lord, and being an effective witness to non-Christian students around them. If you weren't home schooling your children, it was proof-positive that you were grossly unspiritual. It became such a pressure point in this church that if you weren't home schooling your children you did not feel accepted at this church. Families ended up leaving the church because of the pressure they felt on this point. You can only imagine what it would have been like for an un-churched person to show up and try to fit in with this congregation. But that didn't really bother them. They were way too focused on their own "holiness" to worry about whether an unsaved person would be welcome in their church.

They also had, as a congregation, become enamored with the teaching of a man who had become somewhat of a national guru on the subject of childrearing. He held seminars around the nation and taught principles of how to raise your children that were somewhat out of the mainstream. Whether his teaching was helpful or not wasn't the real problem. The problem was that this became another thing they regarded as a matter of holiness. There was no room in their thinking for a Christian to hold a view contrary to what this "expert" taught. If you disagreed with him, you were regarded as unspiritual. If you did not run to attend the seminars he held, you were really lacking in fulfilling your duties as a parent. Al was sure this fellow taught some good principles for parents to follow. He wasn't sure he endorsed everything this man taught but felt there was some good in what he was doing. The folks at Division Street Church made this out to be a matter of overwhelming spiritual importance. They allowed no room for a different opinion on the matter. They measured a person's spirituality by where they stood on this man and his teaching. Al had tried subtly suggesting to some of the people in the church that measuring one's spirituality by things of the world such as this is really a form of worldliness. That went over like a pregnant pole-vaulter! They wouldn't hear of anything like this. They were sure they were right and anyone who thought differently was wrong.

That was the big problem. They had become very proud of their own spirituality and were only too quick to judge that others were not very spiritual at all. It caused them to divide from other believers who just didn't measure up to their exacting standards. Al knew that if there was anything that would hinder the effectiveness of the outreach of the church it was the tendency to divide up over little, unimportant, differences like this. Al muttered to himself, "We already look like a bunch of squabbling school children to the people around us without making it worse by dividing over such secondary issues. This kind of specific rule making on secondary issues also makes us look increasingly weird to the people around us who don't know the Lord." Actually that really didn't bother these super-spiritual Christians. They had come to equate being spiritual with being "different." They had become proud of their holiness to a degree that it didn't bother them that the church was not reaching lost people and thus not growing. They said with real satisfaction, "We are small but we are holy," with the implication that if a church was large it was not holy. It was a known fact, at least in their minds, that if a church was large it just had to have "watered down the gospel." In their view it was a given that small churches were more righteous in the sight of God and large churches were not teaching the truth. There are certainly some ways in which believers must be different than the world around them. But they had made up a bunch of rules that were in addition to the Scriptures and applied them as though they were Holy Writ. For these folks it was almost a virtue to be "odd for God," but it sure didn't help them to reach others.

If Al could just get them to understand that genuine holiness and genuine spirituality is not weird. It is winsome. It is attractive. It doesn't take away from the normal human personality with a lot of rules of what we don't do. It adds to the normal human personality with qualities like love, joy, peace, patience, kindness, and goodness. It makes us better employees, better employers, better husbands, wives, fathers, and mothers. We are better friends, better neighbors, better leaders, and better followers. He wanted them to understand that genuine holiness does not make people look at us and say, "Strange!" It makes people gradually notice over time that we are contented, joyful, kind, and, most importantly of all, have a real purpose for living. In short, most people are attracted to us rather than being turned off by our weirdness. They may not know why they are attracted, but in time most will ask about what makes us different in such a positive way. Genuine holiness holds out hope for the hopeless. Not a hope that they can live up to the standard that we have set, but hope that God can do the same kind of thing in their life as he has done in our life. Real holiness draws people to us. Another word for holiness is godliness. If we are actually like God, to at least some degree, how can that be anything other than attractive to people who desperately need some answers to the deep questions of life?

He tried to warn people that Satan's great desire for Christians is that they become ineffective in the warfare over the souls of lost people. He will do anything to get Christians focused on something other than reaching people who have not yet received Christ as their Savior. He will distract them with problems in their family, their finances, their work, or their health, anything to turn their focus away from reaching un-reached people. He will turn their attention away with luxuries, with hobbies, with all kinds of enjoyable activities, and parties. But, Al reminded people, Satan's favorite strategy is to get Christians focused on substitutes for the real thing. Nowhere is this more effective than in regard to this matter of false holiness. If Satan can get us focused on trying to be holy according to a bunch of man-made rules, he has won the battle. These rules may or may not be bad in themselves, but their effect is almost always destructive. This kind of holiness divides one follower of Christ from others. It creates a kind of spiritual pride that leads to divisions among Christians. Maybe most importantly of all, it ruins our witness for the Lord. It makes us look truly weird to the unbelievers. And all over things that are not essential matters of doctrine or Christian living. If we are going to be effective in our primary calling to make disciples of as many people as we can in the shortest time possible, we can't get distracted by all of this pseudo-holiness. We need to walk close to the Lord in obedience to the things he has clearly commanded us to do and let him develop genuine holiness in us rather than accepting some other person's idea of what holiness is. Now, how in the world was Al going to get the folks at Division Street Church to understand this principle and live according to it?

QUESTIONS FOR REFLECTION

1. What is usually substituted for genuine holiness?
2. How can this make us ineffective in outreach?

WEEK TWO
STUDY GUIDE

1. Have the individual members of the group take a few minutes to reflect on this question: In the last month, what have I clearly been able to apply from the sermon to a practical area of my life? Then report back to the group about what they concluded.

2. Divide the group into groups of three or four. Have each group prepare a charade representing their church's attitude about fellowship. Have each group present their charade to the whole group while the whole group tries to solve their charade.

3. Discuss together the characteristics of true fellowship.

4. Discuss together the phrase, "In worship the only audience is God." How will that affect our commitment to outreach?

5. Divide into groups of three or four, and talk about what is usually substituted for genuine holiness and how that can make us ineffective in outreach.

WEEK THREE

LET SOMEONE ELSE DO IT

IN ONE WAY, WAYNE WAS PROUD OF MISSIONARY CHURCH. For decades they had been leading the way in sending missionaries overseas and supporting them financially. Some of their families had multiple family members, cousins, uncles and aunts, brothers and sisters, and children all serving in one foreign country or the other. This church gave generously to the work overseas. It had gotten to the point that 40 percent of their budget was devoted to overseas work. Their annual missions conference was the highlight of the year for the church. The leaders of the church spent all year planning for this event. It always included missionary speakers, an emphasis on missions in Sunday school, banquets, and a final, very enthusiastic missionary rally. Usually, when the call was extended to those willing to consider serving the Lord in other lands, there were a number who responded, and some of them usually ended up going overseas after suitable preparation. This kind of excellence in foreign missions support had characterized this church for many years and appeared likely to continue for a while longer. If the church itself survived, that is, it might continue for a while longer.

But Wayne knew that was a big *if*! While the church had been very effective in supporting work overseas, it had quietly been in decline for a couple of decades. Now that downward trend had begun to accelerate, and a few people were starting to get a little worried. They were making comments like, "What's happening to our church? It just doesn't seem to be doing very well. Why are there less people in church all the time?" And even, "How can we continue to support our missionaries when the church just keeps getting smaller?"

The problem was really put in bold relief when several of the missionaries came home for their every five years furlough and were shocked by the decline of the church. They also commented that maybe it was time for the church to do some work on the home front, or they wouldn't be able to continue to support missionaries the way they had in the past. The future of the church was not such a sure thing as it had been assumed not that long ago.

"What is the problem here?" is a question that Wayne knew had to be answered because clearly there was an issue that couldn't be ignored for much longer. It seems that the church had allowed itself to become so focused on reaching people in other countries that they had forgotten about reaching people in their own community. Actually, there were a few other churches in Wayne's region with the same trouble. They may not have been such visible examples as Missionary Church, but they had the same problem.

What is the real problem here? Wayne wondered.

The more he looked into this, the more he began to understand. The church had failed to maintain a balance in its ministries, and, more importantly, in the hearts of its people. They had gotten so enthusiastic about reaching lost people in Peru, New Guinea, or Africa that they had forgotten about reaching people in their own community. While it certainly is a good thing to reach people in other countries, it is disobedience to simultaneously fail to reach the people in one's own community. On a more practical level, if people were not reached at home, the church would soon die. If that happened, there would be no ability to send people and support people overseas.

But stop and think about it, Wayne thought. *Isn't it a whole lot easier to send money to support work in another country than to actually share the gospel in your own community? Isn't it a whole lot easier to take a one-week mission trip to Mexico to build a church building than to spend time with your neighbor who doesn't know the Lord and whose lifestyle isn't exactly something you feel comfortable with?*

He understood that the church should continue to support work overseas in obedience to the command of the Lord, but it could not ignore any longer the desperate need to win its own communities and country. It was never the Lord's intention for the church to win people in other countries while not reaching them in their own town or country. He intends for us to reach people everywhere.

This seemed to Wayne to be another case of selfishness rising up in the church. It occurred to him that it doesn't require much personal risk or sacrifice to support missionaries overseas. It is more of a risk to actually attempt to share Christ with real people you will have to see tomorrow and each day thereafter for maybe years to come. But isn't that the whole point? The gospel isn't just presented as some disembodied words. It is presented by a living, breathing fallible human being. To some degree, most people don't come to believe in Jesus until they have at least somewhat come to believe in the person bringing the good news. That doesn't mean the messenger must be living a perfect life. Far from it! But Wayne had observed that when people see that the gospel isn't that we are good enough to merit heaven but that Jesus forgives people who don't deserve forgiveness that is truly good news to them. Our times of failing can actually be great opportunities to share that we do not gain salvation through our own merit but through the grace of God and only through the grace of God. Still, Wayne knew that in most people's minds, it is scarier to share Christ with someone you already know than to send a check to support a missionary overseas. So most people take the easy way out. They pat themselves on the back for supporting missionaries and thereby rationalize their failure to reach their own community and country.

This concerned Wayne greatly. There were enough churches following a similar path in his region that the future didn't look good unless he helped them break this pattern. What would it take to do so? These churches typically gave large amounts of money to the overseas work but devoted very little of their budget to the activities and programs that would reach their own area. They typically sent so much money overseas that they didn't have the money to fund staff positions that would focus on reaching their home area.

He came to realize that it wasn't enough just to talk about changing their programs and their budgets and their staff. What needed to happen first was a change of heart. They needed to see, honestly, that to some degree at least they had been using the emphasis on foreign missions as a rationalization for not reaching their own community. They needed to be brought to a point that they recognized their own disobedience. They needed to see that it wasn't enough to just send money to people who were serving in other countries to obey the Great Commission for them. This "proxy" obedience was only in their minds, not in the mind of the Lord. In reality it was disobedience.

Once again, Wayne saw, Satan's most effective strategy was to create a substitute for true obedience. If Satan could get them to rationalize not reaching their own community by saying, "But look at the great work we are supporting overseas," he would have a rather nifty victory in hand. It didn't hurt that this played right into the desire all of us have to take the easy way out, to do our best to be safe, to take minimal risks, and to exert our efforts doing things that allow us to stay in our comfort zone. It was much more comfortable to plan a missionary banquet that was better than last year's banquet than it was to plan an outreach activity to their own community or to walk across the street to strike up a friendship with a person who was different from them. The work to support missionaries did not require them to interact cross-culturally with people unlike themselves, even though those people lived in their own neighborhood. It was fine for missionaries to do this cross-cultural stuff but not so fine for them to do it themselves. What it came down to, again, was self-interest. These people, including the pastor of the church, were afraid to take the risk of pouring their hearts and their efforts into reaching the people immediately around them. It seemed to them to be an impossible task. Never mind that there were a few churches that were reaching significant numbers of lost people. It seemed to these folks that they would not be able to do the same thing. The risk of failure seemed way higher if they attempted to do in their own town what the missionaries were doing in other countries, and they didn't want to take that risk! They didn't want to look stupid if they fell short of their goals. They were very proud of their accomplishments overseas. They had that work down pat and knew they could do it very well. But reaching their own community was another matter. They might very well fail.

And you know something? Wayne thought to himself. *They probably will fail a few times at first. Trying to learn a new skill always involves a certain amount of trial and error. But so what if they failed a few times? They could learn from each attempt, get back on their feet again, and try a more effective approach next time.* Wayne vowed that he just had to find a way to stimulate this church to broaden the scope of their ministries. He had to get them to see that a failure to reach their own community was disobedience to the Lord, and it would certainly result in the death of this church if they didn't get this turned around. Wayne began to pray specifically for this church that the Lord would open the eyes of the pastor and the other leaders to the reality of what was happening to Missionary Church. He began to pray that this awareness would be followed by a genuine repentance for their disobedience, leading them to greater effectiveness on the home front.

QUESTIONS FOR REFLECTION

1. How might a high level of commitment to overseas missionary work hinder a church's local outreach?

2. How balanced is my church in its commitment to overseas work versus local outreach?

HELP SOMEONE ELSE DO THE WORK

WHEN RICK AND WAYNE BEGAN TO TALK ABOUT MISSIONARY CHURCH AND WHAT WAS AND WAS NOT HAPPENING THERE, RICK REALIZED HE WAS SEEING A VARIATION ON THE MISSIONARY CHURCH PROBLEM IN PARTNERSHIP CHURCH. The focus of this church had gradually developed to the point that it was mainly focused on supporting the work of para-church organizations and para-church missionaries. Para-church ministries are those "alongside" the church doing specialized parts of the overall ministries such as Campus Crusade for Christ, Young Life, Prison Fellowship, and so on. These were valuable ministries to support; they were doing some very good work. People were being led to faith in Christ through these ministries, and some were growing in their faith. What could be wrong with that? Actually, nothing was wrong with it. It was a very good thing, but the problem, like at Missionary Church, was that Partnership Church had focused on these organizations to such an extent that this church was itself in serious decline and would soon die if something didn't change. While the para-church organizations were not doing ministry in other countries, for the most part, they were not leading people to faith in the community around Partnership Church. They, by their own purpose statements, had no intention of trying to duplicate the work of the local church. They directed their efforts to specialized segments of the population such as university students. Rick had himself been very involved in a para-church ministry during his university days and deeply respected the ministries of these organizations.

The problem wasn't that they were not valuable to the overall work of the Lord but that they could not replace the work that only the local church can perform. The local church is focused not on a specialized segment of the population but on the general population at large. The local church, for the most part, is focused on the average, ordinary people who make up the greatest part of the population of most communities. Para-church organizations, for the most part, do not attempt to reach these people. Only the local church devotes itself to reaching and discipling these people, and only the local church is prepared to offer the breadth of ministries required to minister to whole families, not just one segment of families. Most para-church organizations arose out of frustration over the local church's failure to reach people. While they have performed a very valuable ministry to the church at large, they can't replace the ministry of the local church. Most of the leaders of para-church organizations recognize and have a high commitment to the health of congregations doing the work in their own communities. Even they recognize that they can't replace the work of churches.

But just as at Missionary Church, this commitment to the ministries of para-church organizations had gotten out of balance at Partnership Church. The pastor and people had gotten so committed to these ministries that they had neglected the hard work of reaching the average families of their own communities. This imbalance showed up in their budget, their programming, and their staffing. They simply were not committing themselves and their resources to reaching their own communities. The result was that this church was also declining and was in danger of closing its doors at some point in the future. Just like at Missionary Church, the pastor and the people had accepted a substitute for doing the work in their own community. Once again, Satan had succeeded in playing on the desires of people for safety, their comfort zone, minimal risk taking, and taking the path of least resistance. He had led them to rationalize supporting para-church ministries and personnel instead of reaching their own towns. *But*, Rick thought, *what should have happened is a "both and" kind of mentality. They should have both supported para-church ministries and reached their own community. Satan desperately does not want local churches to get serious about their task of reaching the lost people in their own area. He will provide any and every activity that can replace this primary work. If he can succeed in getting the church to fail in their privilege and duty to win people in their own town, his kingdom is secure, and he is delighted.* Rick knew there had to be some way to awaken these churches to the reality of the way they had been hoodwinked by the evil one, and he had better find that way soon before it was too late for these churches.

QUESTIONS FOR REFLECTION

1. What para-church ministries does your church support and get involved in?

2. How is that affecting the church's commitment to local outreach?

ONLY OUR KIND

THERE WERE STILL A FEW "ONLY OUR KIND" CHURCHES LEFT IN AL'S REGION. This had been a much greater problem fifty years ago, but most churches had since moved on and gotten past this issue. However, it had not completely died out. There were still some vestiges of this holding back some of these congregations. It stemmed from pride in their heritage, not a bad thing in itself, but like most things it can become a problem when human nature begins to turn differences into matters of pride. This denomination had begun primarily with German immigrants. The Germans have some great things going for them, including a tremendous work ethic.

No problems with any of that, thought Al. *Be proud of being German. Just don't make it a point of contention with anyone else.*

That was what Al had always said. In the old days of Al's youth, the ethnic heritage had been quite pronounced. Each church service had been conducted half in German and half in English. In those days anyone from outside of this particular ethnic heritage was referred to as *Anglisha* or English. What it really meant was *outsider*. These people tended to socialize pretty much exclusively with people from their own church, and the impression was rather common that they were the ones who had it all figured out spiritually. Those outsiders just didn't quite measure up. Al had grown up thinking that churches who baptized by immersion were really off base. Only after he had gone to college and attended a church from another ethnic background did he start to realize just how much he had been influenced by this very small slice of the whole Christian pie. He began to realize that there were people from many backgrounds who loved the Lord every bit as much as he did but who did things differently than he was used to.

It also became apparent to Al that this problem wasn't limited to just the Germans. He saw churches that were primarily Swedish having a half-joking attitude that you couldn't trust the Norwegians. The people from Greece had their own culturally unique characteristics that they held dear. African Americans and Hispanics clung to their own cultural distinctive to the exclusion of others. There was nothing wrong with being proud of one's cultural heritage. It was actually a good thing until it made one ineffective in reaching other people for Christ. In many of these churches it wasn't enough for a person to accept Christ as one's Savior. The person who came to Christ really ended up being an outsider unless they also accepted the culture of the group which had led them to faith in Jesus. If you were not born into that culture it was a very difficult thing to have to conform to that culture in order to have a relationship with the Lord and a church home which was so essential to one's spiritual survival and growth. Al looked back and nodded knowingly at the fact that the only people who ever accepted Christ through his home church were people from the same ethnic background, primarily children who had grown up in that congregation.

This was true for two primary reasons. First, people from his church rarely socialized with people from other backgrounds. There was a cultural barrier to prevent them from sharing with other people. Al knew that most people come to Christ in the context of relationships that have been established and cultivated over time. He understood that very few people accept Christ the first time they hear the gospel. Most people decide to follow Christ after they have heard the gospel several times, in several different ways, from several different people. If our only method of presenting the gospel is confrontational, "whacking strangers with the gospel," we won't be very effective. It is most effective if all believers are deliberately cultivating authentic relationships with those who don't yet believe. In those relationships we are to love them in real, practical, helpful ways, not just see them as a "notch on our gun belt." One deterrent to building these relationships is that sometimes the people we are trying to reach will be living in a way that we wouldn't feel comfortable living ourselves. *Well*, Al thought, *what do we expect? We can't expect people who don't know the Lord to live in any way other than being controlled by the world, the flesh, and the devil. They don't have any choice about that until the Lord sets them free to live with his power and freedom. We are the ones who need to accept them as they are if we have any hope of reaching them for the Lord. If they accept Christ he will begin the work of transformation in their life. It isn't up to us to require this of them before they can believe in him.*

The second reason Al had seen for the churches with a strong cultural heritage having a hard time reaching anyone who is not from their background is that there is an unspoken, and sometimes spoken, realization that if a person comes to faith in Jesus they will be expected to adopt the cultural characteristics of that church. People who are being approached with the gospel are usually aware of those cultural characteristics and feel like they don't fit even before they accept Christ. They are not sure they will be able to—or even want to—conform to these unique characteristics. So there is a barrier that must be overcome even before they will consider the gospel. It is an additional and completely unnecessary hurdle that prevents people from coming to faith in Jesus.

Thankfully, today most of the churches with strong ethnic backgrounds have moved, at least somewhat, away from those ethnic cultural issues that may present a barrier to people coming to faith in Jesus. But, sadly, what Al saw developing in churches today is new cultural characteristics that have nothing to do with ethnic background. They are, nevertheless, presenting barriers to the presentation of the gospel and to people coming to faith in Jesus. A local church develops its own cultural "flavor" that soon becomes a large part of what that church is about. Again, it's not wrong for a church to have unique characteristics, so long as they don't present barriers to the presentation of the gospel and to people coming to faith in Christ. One of those characteristics might be with regard to the style of worship. Each church needs to take a very careful look at what a Sunday morning attending our church would feel like to the unchurched person. Often we have things in our services that are not required or even encouraged by the Scriptures that feel downright weird to the person who is not from our background. Al wanted to encourage every pastor or lay leader to try hard to put themselves in the shoes of the truly un-churched person and take a hard look at the Sunday morning experience at their church from that perspective. He wanted to encourage them to remove anything that was not required by the Scriptures but would make the un-churched person uncomfortable.

Another way Al had seen this come into play is when a church develops characteristics that are not required or even encouraged by the Scriptures that make the members seem too "different" when they are out mingling with the people of the community. Sometimes this is something as simple as unique verbal expressions that seem perfectly normal to the regular church attendees but seem strange to the person who doesn't attend the church. Another thing that can come across as weird is if the church encourages its people to follow a schedule that, while not required by the Bible, makes them seem out of place in the society around them. They frequently say "no" to the people around them who would like to spend time with them. The church attendee just doesn't have time for this because the church requires or encourages them to spend so many evenings in church activities that they have no time to spend with their un-churched neighbors.

Al knew that another serious issue to consider in all this was the fact that sometimes these cultural characteristics led to divisions between believers. Al had seen too many cases in which the folks from Church A don't hang out much with the folks from Church B because there are so many differences between them on non-essential matters that they just don't feel comfortable with each other. They sometimes even end up competing with each other for the opportunity to win a certain person to the Lord. Al understood that this is totally confusing to people who have not yet come to faith. They can't understand why Christians from one church don't get along with Christians from another church. If Christians from one church speak poorly about another church, it is a real turn off to un-churched people. Even they understand that if we all name the same Lord we certainly should have better relationships with each other. They know that we should see each other as all being on the same team. Al remembered how, when he was growing up, people from one church hardly spoke to people from the other churches in town. They all seemed to think that they were the only ones who were doing things the way the Lord really wanted them done. "It is time for the people of God to get out of their ethnic ghettos and start playing on the same team," Al exhorted people whenever he got the chance. "We need to deliberately set aside our differences and consciously choose to work together."

Al hoped that one way this would show up is that it would heal the racial divide. Both whites and non-whites are guilty of creating and cultivating the divide. It isn't exclusively the fault of white people. People from other races often feel more comfortable staying within their culture than making the changes to create a cooperative atmosphere. *But for the sake of the Lord's work in America,* he thought, *both sides are going to have to make the sacrifices that will allow us to work together in a fully cooperative way. At the heart of all this business of keeping away from each other, of clinging to unnecessary cultural characteristics, is selfishness and fear. We want to stay safe and comfortable. It is just a whole lot easier to stay in our own enclave than it is to, for the sake of the powerful spread of the gospel, change things about us and our church. Things that are preventing us from reaching more people and from being more effective in cooperating with other believers for the sake of the gospel must be removed if we are going to become more effective.*

QUESTIONS FOR REFLECTION

1. Most of us don't live in "ethnic ghettos" anymore. Are there some "cultural ghettos" your church might be living in?

2. Are there "unique" things about your church that might be a turn-off for an un-churched person?

OUT OF STEP

HERITAGE CHURCH WAS A GROUP OF PEOPLE WHO WERE PROUD OF THEIR PAST. They had been a great church in the 1950s and 1960s. In fact they had been regarded as the flagship church for the Rocky Mountain Region. Rick had heard many stories of their glory days. They had been the first church of their denomination to be started in their city over 110 years ago, and there was much to be proud of. They did have a rich history, but the present was another matter. For the last forty years, the church had been in a gradual decline. For the last fifteen years that decline had accelerated alarmingly. It was clear that unless something was done the church would close its doors in the near future. The thing that was quite surprising was that there were a significant number of people in the church who were in deep denial. They wouldn't even admit that the church was shrinking. When confronted with this truth they would say, "Oh, we're doing okay. We are holding our own." This was in spite of the fact that the church had shrunk from a peak of five hundred in attendance to its present one hundred. Rick was very concerned that they would not wake up in time and would simply ride this church into the ground all the while declaring that they were doing okay.

Rick had a pretty clear understanding of why this church was in such steep decline. They had simply refused to keep up with the changing world around them. They were still doing things the way they did them in the 50s and 60s when the church had been at its peak. They were a silent warning of the dangers of trying to keep things the same. This was clear in the music that was the standard fare in the church. The instruments were limited to the piano and a once-grand pipe organ. The songs were hymns that had been around the church for centuries or classical music more suited to another era. Rick loved the singing of hymns, as well as their message, but he also recognized that for the un-churched person this music was a completely foreign cultural experience. People out in the world beyond the church doors simply did not listen to pipe organ music. The hymn singing was a sound that people out in the culture just didn't hear, except when a TV program or movie showed a church from the old west days. Then this music was seen as a quaint relic of by-gone days.

But the people of this church had made this kind of music into a matter of spiritual correctness. They could not see it as just a matter of their preferences. They made it a matter of right and wrong. They spoke of the newer Christian music that was being written today as "trash." They regarded the music of today as a threat to the church. They were concerned that the church at large would "lose its heritage" if any music other than hymns and classical music was used in the church. Never mind that the music they thought was so critical to the future of the church had all been "new" music at one time. Some of the hymns they so cherished had come about when Christian leaders of that day had put Christian words to tavern tunes. It was common for those who wrote hymns or other such music to adapt a popular tune or a classical piece to suit the needs of their song. These had been the original "contemporary Christian" music. They had been very contemporary to the culture in which the church existed at the time of their writing. And that was the whole point of their writing. The hymns of Wesley and Whitfield had been reviled by the established church at the time of their writing because they were "contemporary" to the culture of the day. Now these people today regarded them as the only "righteous" kind of music. They were, for the most part, completely unaware of the origins of these songs and the purpose for which they had been written. They had been written to be of interest to and understandable to the un-churched people of the day. The musical scores had originated in the secular music of the day. The musical sounds were indistinguishable from the secular music of the day. That was, after all, the purpose for which the writers had come up with these songs. They did not want the un-churched person to have to adopt the culture of the church, a foreign culture to them, in order to accept Christ as their Savior, so they wrote songs that fit the secular culture of the day.

America is increasingly becoming a foreign culture to Christians, thought Rick, *but we are expecting un-churched people to accept our culture before they accept Christ as their Savior. Any effective foreign missionary has understood that the gospel has to be presented in a way that is relevant to the culture of the people the missionary is trying to reach.* Rick's older brother was a missionary in Papua, New Guinea for twenty-three years. He didn't go to the people there wearing a suit and tie, and he didn't live in a two-story colonial house. He wore considerably less than a suit and tie and lived in a grass thatched hut like the people he was trying to reach. Occasionally a "missionary barrel" would come and some of the native people would be wearing American clothes for a while, but this didn't last long. *The missionary doesn't change the theological content of the gospel but does present it in ways that are appealing to and relevant to the culture,* thought Rick. *Since America is increasingly becoming a culture that is foreign to Christians, a desire to be an effective witness requires that we present the gospel in culturally relevant ways without changing its theological content.*

Rick understood this principle. In the churches he pastored, his stated desire was for the worship band in his church to rival the best nightclub bands in the city in the style and quality of their music. It wasn't that Rick liked to frequent nightclubs or had grown up listening to this music in church. Quite to the contrary, it had been an adjustment for him to get used to this kind of music in the church. He had grown up singing only hymns and loved to sing hymns. He loved to raise his voice praising God by singing hymns—in other words, "belting out" the hymn. He really loved singing the bass line in the chorus of "It Is Well with My Soul." He had also grown up loving the sounds of Creedence Clearwater Revival and Simon and Garfunkel, but had not thought that such a sound had a place in the church. It had taken him a while to get used to the idea of using such secular sounding music in the church. But once he understood the purpose for doing this and saw how effective it was in enabling the church to reach un-churched people, he had fallen in love with the newest Christian contemporary music.

It was clear to Rick that this applies to more than just music. In everything that is a matter of style preference, when the Bible has not given us a command or prohibition in the matter, the church should fit the style of the culture around it. If the church is going to be effective in America, it must again return to its missionary roots and start adapting to the culture in which it exists. "There are biblical absolutes that we dare not ever compromise, but there are many parts of our behavior that have nothing to do with biblical commands. They are just a matter of our preferences, and we must sacrifice our preferences for the sake of effectively presenting the gospel," was the message Rick wanted people to understand. Style preferences change with every generation. The church must be prepared to adapt to these issues in each generation. For example, the clothes we wear. Churches in which the expectation is that every man and boy will wear a coat and tie every Sunday and every woman and girl will wear a dress must look very weird to the secular culture around them. *Where else in our culture do whole families dress like that for anything other than a wedding or funeral? Why would Christians want to appear weird to non-Christians in such a non-essential matter?* Rick thought. *We must likewise be careful of the language we use. Do you think that calling each other "brother" and "sister" makes us look a little like a cult in the eyes of the world? It is true that we are brothers and sisters in the Lord, but there is nothing in the Scriptures that requires us to use that expression to address each other. We don't even find the Christians in the Bible addressing each other in that way.* Rick didn't find anywhere in the Bible where Paul is called "Brother Paul" or Peter, "Brother Peter."

Rick repeatedly taught that Christians need to look at everything they do through the eyes of the un-churched person. Anything that might appear strange or confusing to a non-Christian should be given a very careful examination. If the Bible requires us to maintain that behavior, by all means, we must maintain it. But if the Bible doesn't require it, then it is just a matter of our preference. He tried to get people to understand that *if we are passionate about reaching lost people, we will sacrifice our preferences for the sake of effectiveness in evangelism.* We expect that missionaries in foreign countries will do this in order to be effective in their cause. What we must realize is that, increasingly, we are living in a culture that is foreign to the Christian culture. One reason the culture has become resistant to the Christian message is that we have so often insisted on maintaining a Christian sub-culture that is not a matter of biblical command. It is purely a matter of our preferences and our traditions.

He knew that in every period of great revival in the church there has been great effectiveness in reaching lost people. Not surprisingly, these have also been times in which a great deal of new "contemporary" Christian music has been written. They have also been times of new innovations in methods in order to fit the culture. The established church of the day rejected John Wesley's passion to reach lost people and his style. So what did Wesley do? He began to use totally new methods. He started preaching in open fields to crowds of people who were regarded as not suitable to attend the established church. Soon a great revival was sweeping over the British Empire. That revival resulted in great social change including the abolition of slavery and regulating the use of child labor that had exploded as a result of the industrial revolution. The church must be prepared to adapt to the culture surrounding each new generation.

In our day, the sudden rise of the Internet and the postmodern idea that there are no absolutes present huge challenges to the church. The church will have to be relevant to a culture in which these realities dominate people's lives in a massive way. Rick wrestled with the reality that the church will have to change methods to adapt to the digital age or risk not being heard at all. The church will have to learn to communicate the gospel in ways that take into consideration that the vast majority of Americans do not believe that there is such a thing as absolute truth. Its approach to evangelism will have to change. Far too many churches seem to think we are still living in a culture in which most people had a basically positive view of Christians and some basic understanding of the simplest truths of the Bible. In reality, we live in a culture that is becoming increasingly, and bitterly, anti-Christian. Most of the people in America now probably have as much understanding of Islam as they do of basic truths of the Christian faith. If the church doesn't change its way of doing church, it will soon be increasingly persecuted.

Rick knew that if the church expects the Lord to work in powerful ways again, if it longs for a great awakening to sweep the land again, it will have to stop clinging to its traditional ways of doing things. It was clear to Rick that the main reasons Christian people cling to the way they have been doing things are comfort, selfishness, and fear. They are comfortable doing things the way they always have, and they don't want to give up that comfort. They are selfish. They want things the way they want things, and they really don't care that by clinging to their traditional ways of doing things they are failing to reach unreached people. In essence, they are saying to those who don't know the Lord, "If you don't want to adopt our ways you can just go to hell." None of them would admit that, but in reality that is what they are saying.

Rick knew that too many church people are saying, in essence, "We are afraid to try something new. It seems too risky. What if we fail?" Rick's thought was that a little failure never killed anyone. Failure is usually the start of learning how to succeed. All the great accomplishers throughout history have had a number of failures before they arrived at the success for which they are so well known. For Christians who are steeped in a more traditional approach to doing church, this will be a learning process. They will make some mistakes along the way while learning to adapt their style and methods in order to become more effective in the battle for the deliverance of souls from Satan's clutches. But they can learn from those mistakes and continue on to a wonderful result.

Rick wanted to call out to these people, "Just give it a try! Face the reality of our massive, ongoing failure to fulfill the Great Commission. Repent in great sorrow for our disobedience to the Lord's command. Let's give up our comfort, safety, and selfishness for the sake of reaching lost people!"

Rick was concerned that some Christians are so worried about "preserving our heritage" as though our heritage is all about the style of music and worship and Christian subculture. Rick tried to say to them, "The heritage we really want to be concerned about preserving is the first century heritage of adapting our style and methods to the culture around us so that we become very effective in reaching lost people again. Why would we want to preserve a heritage of behavior that has resulted in the rapid decline in Christianity over the last one hundred years in America? That is not a heritage we should be proud of, and we certainly do not want to promulgate that kind of behavior. We don't want to hold up that heritage as a model for our children and for young Christians to admire. We should be repenting of that behavior and apologizing for that heritage, not holding it up as our ideal."

"May God bring us back to a heritage of effectively reaching many lost people," was Rick's prayer.

QUESTIONS FOR REFLECTION

1. Try real hard to imagine being a truly un-churched person attending your church's worship service. What in the service would seem "weird" to that person?

2. What will it take for your church to be culturally relevant to the un-churched people you are most likely to reach? In other words, people who are most socio-economically like the people of the church?

WEEK THREE
STUDY GUIDE

1. As a group, discuss the questions: How strong is our church's commitment to overseas missionary work? How strong is our church's commitment to local outreach?

2. Have individual members of the group make a rough drawing representing any "cultural ghetto" characteristics of your church. Have each person describe the meaning of their drawing to the whole group.

3. Break into groups of three or four and have each group summarize a comparison of the culture in which your church was founded with the culture now surrounding the church. Report back to the whole group. Do the people of your church fit the demographic profile of the people around the church?

4. Discuss what changes your church would have to make to fit the culture of the neighborhood around the church.

5. Have each group member observe your church's worship service next Sunday through the eyes of a truly un-churched person. Report back to the group next week about how it would have felt for an un-churched person to sit through the worship service.

WEEK FOUR

NON-ESSENTIALS

CHURCHES LIKE "CHURCH BY THE WAY" REALLY IRRITATED WAYNE. They were so sure that the way they did things was the right way. There was no hesitation on their part to condemn other churches that varied from their way of doing things. They readily crossed off whole denominations as falling short of God's expectations because they didn't "see the light" according to their way of doing things. They even hinted that Wayne was missing out on God's best for him, and there was talk that they might leave the denomination this region was part of. What really bugged Wayne was the fact that the things about which they were making such major issues were really minor issues. They were small things that were a matter of their preferences rather than a matter of biblical mandates. Wayne knew that the problem with this approach was that these people treated their preferences as though they were absolutes of the Scriptures and had divided from Christian brothers over things like style of preaching, style of music, and expressions of the gifts of the Spirit. Wayne knew that these things were not essentials and they had better stop treating them as though they were.

This attitude about the church and Christian living focuses on non-essentials like which model of doing church is godlier. These Christians are usually very concerned that the seeker-driven model of doing church falls short of God's expectations. They think that it waters down the gospel. Actually they regard it as being doctrinally in error. Sometimes Christians attending a seeker-driven church become just as self-righteous about their way of doing church and regard everyone else as failing to do God's will. All the while they are ignoring that there are some important things to learn from the new, more mission-minded churches. But Wayne knew, if they were honest about things, they would have to admit that with the condition of the church in America all of the models of doing church were failing. None of them were completely the answer. If any one model was the answer, if any one model was thoroughly doing the job of fulfilling the Great Commission of winning people to faith in Jesus and teaching them to obey all that Jesus taught, the church would not be in the terrible state of decline it was in.

Rick recognized that all the models are to some degree failing. To put it in the simplest of words, the Great Commission has two halves: winning people to faith in Jesus and training them to live lives of obedience to our Lord. The seeker-driven model is at least winning people to faith in Jesus. It has failed to some degree in discipling them to become obedient followers of Jesus, but at least it has won them to faith. The traditional model is, for the most part, failing to fulfill both halves of the Great Commission. It isn't winning many people to believe in Jesus, so there aren't new believers to train to live obedient lives. None of the sides in this debate has any room for self-righteousness. *The point is,* Rick felt, *we should not be wasting our breath debating these points. We should be saving our breath for the really hard work of reaching lost people and training them to live lives of obedience to the Lord.*

Rick believed that the tragedy of this approach has two parts. First it divides sincere Christian brothers from other sincere Christian brothers. When we are divided over non-essentials like this, the non-Christian world looks at us and holds their noses, for very good reasons. The second part of this tragedy flows out of the first. When we divide over non-essentials like this it makes ineffective the witness of the church as a whole. We all get labeled as a bunch of hypocrites who can't get along with each other. Of course, Satan loves nothing more than when we give him one more thing to whisper in the minds of those who don't believe. He says to them, "See? Those Christians are all a bunch of hypocrites. They can't even get along with each other. God sure doesn't seem to have made much difference in their lives or their relationships."

Rick was so frustrated that Christians are arguing with each other over things like church polity, the charismatic gifts of the Spirit, what style of worship to practice, what music is best in the church, and a whole host of non-essential issues. These things are not completely unimportant, but they certainly are not important enough to divide from sincere, well-meaning brothers and sisters in Christ.

"Let's keep things in perspective," was what Wayne wanted to counsel these Christians in these churches. "These are not life and death matters. Intelligent Christians have differed on these points for centuries. Why do we want to waste our time and our opportunity to spread the gospel by squabbling over these things?" It was both telling and to be expected that these churches were not growing. They were not growing because they were not reaching people with the gospel, and they were not reaching people with the gospel for several reasons. It was obvious to Rick that one reason was that reaching people was not their focus. They were so focused on making sure they and everybody else were doing things exactly the way they thought things should be done, they had no time or energy to focus on outreach. Secondly, even if they had put some energy into outreach, they would have proven ineffective because they had created for themselves such a bad reputation in their community. Also, their contentious spirit would have manifested itself quite readily to the people they were trying to reach. *Who is going to give a serious listen to the gospel*, Rick thought, *when it comes packaged in the form of a human wolverine? The gospel is most readily heard when it comes from a person who manifests a winsome spirit. When a person is as contentious and divisive as these folks are it shows on one's face. That kind of countenance scares people off before they even get a chance to hear of the love God has for them.*

Sadly, these folks were not going to listen to Wayne or anyone else who didn't fully support their peccadilloes. The ones who most needed to accept input from an objective third party were the least likely to receive that kind of input. Wayne felt it had come to the point that all he could realistically do was to pray for this congregation. He prayed that the sovereign Lord of the universe would break through their self-righteousness even if it meant the church would have to go through some hard times.

QUESTIONS FOR REFLECTION

1. Is there anything about which the members of your church have a tendency to be "self-righteous"?

2. How might these things affect the truly un-churched people you hope to reach?

WORSHIPING OUR HISTORY

RICK LOVED GOING TO VISIT FIRST CHURCH. Their building was absolutely gorgeous! It had been built in the early nineteen hundreds and had that classic look and feel. It was so restful to sit in the sanctuary. It engendered such a feeling of worship. Generations of families had been born, grew up, married, dedicated their children, and had their funerals in this church building. It had many precious memories for many people. The problem was the building had become an albatross. The neighborhood around the church had changed so much that the existing congregation really had no hope of being able to reach this area. It would have required a complete reinvention of the church, to be like the culture of the surrounding area, to reach this neighborhood, and that wasn't likely to happen.

While a relocation to a new neighborhood is not the answer in every case, to Rick it sure appeared that it was the best answer for First Church. These old "First Churches" usually fall into a very predictable pattern. Rick saw that in most cases the neighborhood had changed around them so significantly that the church had been on a slow path of decline. The decline had accelerated rapidly in the last ten to twenty years. They were not reaching the people in their neighborhood and, consequently, the church was shrinking. These churches really had only three choices. If they chose to continue doing what they were doing, without making major changes, the church would die. The rate of decline would get faster with every passing year, and their demise would soon come. Their second option was to change their ministries, their approach, and their style radically to fit the neighborhood around them. If it had become a Hispanic neighborhood they need to hire a Spanish-speaking pastor, develop ministries to reach Hispanic people, and start having worship services much more in a Hispanic style of worship. If it had become a Russian neighborhood, an African American neighborhood, or a poor Anglo neighborhood or, rarely, a very affluent neighborhood, the church would need to change itself to fit the people now surrounding the church. Very few of these churches had enough of the kind of people willing to make such radical changes that they can pull off the second alternative. One thing that made this kind of change so difficult is that, typically in these churches, the majority of the members of the congregation no longer lived in the neighborhoods around the church. Most of them were driving a considerable distance in from the suburbs to attend the church. It is a great deal harder for a church to reach a neighborhood that their own members don't live in. To be able to have much hope of reaching the neighborhood around the church, many of those same people would have to move in from the suburbs to the neighborhood around the church and develop their primary friendships and relationships in that neighborhood. That was very unlikely to happen. For those churches that can make the radical changes to minister to the neighborhood they now find themselves surrounded by, Rick said, "Blessings on them. Let's encourage them in any way we can." But, realistically, most churches will not be able to make these changes.

Rick knew that this left only one realistic option for most of these churches. They needed to sell their current property and buy new property in a neighborhood closer to a demographic match for the people who made up the church. The attendees of the church already lived in these areas. They already had their friendships and primary relationships in these areas. They already spoke the cultural language of these areas. It wouldn't be such a cross-cultural stretch for the people of the church to communicate with the people who already lived in these neighborhoods. Whenever Rick or someone else suggested the idea of relocating, there were those who proclaimed loudly that the church couldn't abandon this neighborhood, that it should reach the area it was already in. But the problem was that it wasn't reaching the neighborhood now. In reality, it had already abandoned the neighborhood and had no realistic hope of reaching the people around them. The pastor of First Church had actually led a prostitute to the Lord from the area around the church. This woman had called in to one of the TV ministries, and they had recommended that she call First Church. When she did, the pastor had her come in to his office, and he led her to the Lord. But the problem was, the people of the church felt so uneasy around her that she didn't feel at all comfortable attending church. She ended up slipping back into her old lifestyle. The people of the church were simply not emotionally equipped to minister to the realities of the area around the church.

After agonizing over this for a number of years, Rick concluded that to reach these older areas of a city required a ministry focused on being adapted to the real needs of the area. It was much more effective to start such a ministry from the ground up than to try to convert an existing church into this type of ministry. He believed that if we have a great desire to reach the older parts of the city, we will develop this kind of new ministry and encourage a number of churches to band together to support it.

Rick had discovered that a problem arose whenever an old First Church faced the needed to relocate to even survive. There is such loyalty to the building itself. There are so many great memories that people have of events that occurred in the building, and it is such a beautiful building. People have such an emotional attachment to the building itself that they would almost rather see the church die than leave the building. In the majority of these churches, the church actually did die, and the building either sat empty or was sold to someone else anyway. How much better to be proactive and make the moves to become an effective church that is actively reaching people, even if it is doing so in a new area!

Rick began proposing a different approach. He began teaching church leaders and pastors, "Buildings are just tools—nothing more, nothing less. We need good buildings, good tools, but we have got to stop revering them as 'sacred places.' There is nothing sacred or holy about the building itself. An elementary school gymnasium, when the church is meeting there, is every bit as sacred as the beautiful, one-hundred-year old, sanctuary of First Church. The Christians of the first century sometimes met in the catacombs, in Jewish Synagogues, or even outdoors." Rick had seen a beautiful worship service being conducted under a large tree in Africa.

The problem Rick repeatedly encountered is that it is so easy to slip into what almost equals worship of the building itself. *When that happens, we stop seeing the building as a tool, and the building itself begins to control our decisions regarding ministry. Soon the building is preventing effective ministry instead of being a tool to enhance ministry,* Rick thought. Rick knew that this was going to be a long battle to get people to start seeing church buildings as just tools, but he was determined to win that battle. He was just too frustrated seeing churches destroying the future of their ministry because they had made their building into something much more than just a tool.

Rick began to teach congregations, when he had the opportunity, that they had to start thinking differently about their buildings. He encouraged them to assume that, in all areas but small towns, the buildings will have a limited life span. He tried to instruct them that church buildings would not be effective tools, enabling effective ministries for more than fifty years. They would probably have an even shorter effective life than that. After that, if the congregation continued to cling to the building, it would become a hindrance to the ministry—not a help. So they would need to assume that the building would serve them for no more than fifty years and then need to be sold so the church could relocate.

We are "pilgrims and strangers in this land," Rick thought, *and it hinders our ministry when we try to erect buildings that are more than just tools. There is such a powerful tendency, when we plan and construct a building, to expect that a hundred years from now, or even more it will still be a powerful witness in the community. That thinking is just not based on reality. An honest look around the church scene in this country will quickly make clear that there are very few church buildings of one hundred years in age that still house a vibrant ministry. Most old church buildings are empty shells.*

Rick began to try to find an opportunity to speak to all churches, or at least their building committees, that were considering a new church building. He began encouraging them to adopt this more realistic attitude about the longevity of the church buildings. This had several significant implications. One was that before the new structure was begun, in the planning phases, thought must be given to the day when it would be sold so the church could move on with its ministry. Rick began to encourage churches to not saddle the next generation with a building that would severely limit their ministry. This would require that the land and building could be relatively easily sold for a use other than a church. Probably this meant that a church should seek to have the land zoned for a commercial use before construction began. It also meant that the building needed to be designed with a future commercial use in mind. It should not be a building that was so "churchy" in its design that it could not have any future use for commercial purposes. It would need to be a "free-span" type of structure so that walls could be removed or added with relative ease. It would need to avoid the type of sanctuary that could only possibly be used for worship, not any commercial use. It was necessary that all rooms be designed so that they could be easily adapted for other uses.

Sometimes folks would object that the church wouldn't even look like a church building, but Rick knew this was not the case. He had seen some beautiful worship spaces that were actually multi-purpose rooms. When the padded stacking chairs were removed, the room served quite nicely as a gymnasium and fellowship hall. But it had a permanent platform for the worship activities and, when set up for worship, was a very attractive worship space. If the need arose in the future for this building to be used for another type of use, it could be easily converted to a more commercial enterprise without spending a fortune to make the conversion.

Rick also knew that it was going to be important for the people designing and constructing the facility to explain to the congregation that this was the plan for the building. They would need to continue to communicate this reality to the church people on a periodic basis so that even twenty-five years later people would understand that this was not going to be the permanent home of the congregation. All budgeting would be done with the view in mind that the day would arrive when the building would be sold so the church could move to an area in where they would be much more effective. Rick prayed regularly that all the teaching he was doing on this subject would end up being a blessing to future generations. He realized that he probably wouldn't be around to see the benefits of this strategy, but he felt it was so important to the future of these churches that he was willing to risk the hassles of trying to teach congregations this bit of future thinking. Maybe, just maybe, there would be a church or two that would not find its future ministry stifled by an emotional over-commitment to a building that had been designed and constructed many decades before. If that happened even fifty years hence, Rick knew that it would have been worth all the effort he was putting forth and the risk he was taking now.

QUESTIONS FOR REFLECTION

1. Do the people in your church fit the demographic profile of the people around the church?

2. What changes would your church have to make to fit the culture of the neighborhood around the church?

WHAT HAVE WE LEARNED?

IT WAS ABOUT SIX MONTHS BEFORE RICK, AL, AND WAYNE WERE ABLE TO GET TOGETHER AGAIN. They shared what had been happening in their lives and rejoiced that Rick's wife, Marilyn, had recovered so well from surgery. They continued to pray for Al's son, Matt, who, as yet, was continuing to show no interest in trusting the Lord as his Savior and was continuing to put his trust in the common thinking of the society around him.

They compared notes on what they had been learning and concluding regarding the frustrations of trying to help their churches grow. What could they do to make a difference? They agreed on the most common reasons why churches were in decline, but how could they change things? Maybe if they helped church leaders see the causes of decline, these leaders would begin to reverse some of these trends. After a few hours of poring over what they had learned, they concluded that maybe Rick should be the first to start bringing their conclusions to the churches in his region.

Rick went home and began to summarize all they had learned in a way that he could present clearly to churches. When he had it organized to the point that he felt confident he could give a coherent explanation of what they had come to understand, the three of them began to pray that God would open a door for Rick to begin to teach this material. An opportunity arose when Bethany Church in Rick's region called and asked him to meet with their board for a long-range planning session. With a little fear and trepidation, he agreed to meet with them in three weeks. It was time to put up or shut up! He wondered how this would all be received, but he had to take this opportunity to try to make a difference. That Saturday he drove into the church parking lot with nerves on full alert. This was what they had been praying for. Now was the time to make it happen.

Rick walked into the meeting room and greeted each board member warmly as they straggled in to take their places. They loaded up on coffee and bagels and sat down to begin what they secretly feared would be a boring exercise in futility. Rick wasted no time once he was given the floor.

He began, "Gentlemen and ladies, three of us regional superintendents have spent the last two years wrestling with the question of why so many churches in our three regions are either at a plateau or declining. We, after much discussion and prayer, have concluded that there are thirteen primary reasons for the decline of our churches." He then fired up his PowerPoint presentation and began to relate these reasons:

1. The Consumer Approach
2. The Risk Free Approach
3. The Suspicion of Leadership Approach
4. The Academic Approach
5. The Fellowship Approach
6. The Worship Approach
7. The Holiness Approach
8. The Foreign Missions Approach
9. The Para-Church Approach
10. The Ethnic Emphasis Approach
11. The No Cultural Relevancy Approach
12. The Arguing Over Non-essentials Approach
13. The Worship of the Building Approach

"The Consumer Mentality has come to characterize almost all the people attending the churches in the region," Rick began. "The feeling that the church exists to serve its members is so prevalent that it dominates the churches. The people think that their role is to consume the services the church is obligated to provide. Of course, when this thinking prevails there is almost no emphasis placed on reaching out to lost people. In the minds of the people this isn't why the church exists. It exists to take care of the people who are already there. In most churches evangelism wouldn't even make the top ten priorities. If the church doesn't win the people of its generation, it will cease to exist. In the current generation, only 4 percent of the American population is putting their faith in Jesus. Christianity is on the decline all over this country."

Rick went on to explain the next reason the church is dying in this country. He pointed out how the church has come to value the "voice of reason" over the "voice of faith." He showed them from the Scriptures that God is not pleased unless we live a life of walking by faith. He explained the chart detailing the difference between walking by faith and walking by sight. It was a natural next step to point out that unless they attempted things that were humanly impossible, they really didn't need God to be involved in their endeavor. They could do it themselves even if the Lord didn't do anything on their behalf. He reminded them of the heroes of the faith who trusted God to part the Red Sea, keep them safe in a lions' den, and empower them to preach the gospel throughout the hostile Roman Empire. These were the people they were to emulate, not the person who routinely counseled caution. Yet the churches kept putting people who were so cautious as to rule out any bold steps of faith into positions of leadership. That made a few of these board members squirm in their seats, but it needed to be said.

Most of these board members had grown up in the sixties and seventies when the watchword of the culture was "trust no one in a leadership position." This philosophy had found a receptive home in the church. There was a widely accepted view that the pastor shouldn't be leading the church. That wasn't supposed to be his job. Rick drew their attention to the biblical pattern that showed that whenever God wanted something done He raised up an individual to lead that effort. The Lord virtually never gave a new vision of what was to be done by speaking to the people as a whole. He didn't even choose to speak through a committee. He raised up one person, implanted the vision in the heart of that person, then told him to go lead the people in the fulfilling of that vision. Often the people chose to reject the message and messenger the Lord had sent. Sometimes they even stoned the prophet, but God continued to use the same method. Rick helped them see that even in the things God had done powerfully in their day he had followed this same pattern. The board members were those who struggled most with this principle and engaged Rick in a lively debate over this principle which was so contrary to their belief system. But Rick gave calm biblical answers to their questions. In the end, there seemed to be some grudging assent to this point, so Rick moved on to his next issue.

"Way too many churches across the country have fallen into this trap," Rick said. "It is partly a result of the teaching espoused in seminaries that the pastor's most important job is to teach the Bible accurately. In this view, nothing else even comes close to the importance of this task. It is as though both people and pastor agree that if he just did a good job of transferring Bible facts from his brain to theirs, everything else would fall into place.

"And of course," Rick emphasized, "the pastor teaching the Bible accurately is very important to the life of the church. Without a biblical foundation, the people would be led into all kinds of harmful extremes."

Rick also helped them understand that an equally important role of the pastor was to lead the people in becoming obedient to the Word. He was instructed in the Bible to "reprove, rebuke, and exhort" the people. This goes beyond just teaching Bible facts. It actually holds people accountable to obey what was taught. Nowhere was this more lacking than in the area of the effective evangelism of the church. The great majority of the churches in the country were characterized by an attitude that if the pastor just taught Bible facts accurately they could all go home satisfied. But no one was sounding the clarion call to the troops, "Let's go batter down Satan's gates and set his captives free." It was even assumed that if the pastor just taught his people accurately they would do evangelism. The problem was, this kind of teaching did not automatically result in effective evangelism. None of the people on that board could point to an example of a single church that followed the motto of "just teach the people" that was reaching any significant number of lost people.

By now the members of the board of Bethany Church were feeling pretty uncomfortable, yet slowly admitting that Rick had hit home on these matters.

"Next is a point that I think you can all relate to." Rick began his presentation of another reason why churches are in decline. "Most of our churches have a major emphasis on fellowship," he continued. "And why not? Most of what church members consider fellowship is really just having fun with their friends. It doesn't get into real fellowship, which can only be experienced 'in the foxhole' of combat. It is a cheap substitute for the real thing. Real fellowship holds one another accountable to obedience to all the commands of Jesus, most especially the command to make disciples of as many people as we possibly can. It is only as we are fully engaged in the battle for which the church has been left here on earth that we really experience true fellowship. But most churches know nothing of this kind of real fellowship. They are selfishly choosing to get all wrapped up in this pseudo fellowship, which is really nothing more than just hanging out with their friends. They have spiritualized this to the point that they regard it as a Biblical mandate and woe to the person who in any way suggests that it isn't the most important reason for the church to exist. Pastors risk their tenure as the pastor of these churches when they dare to suggest that all this emphasis on 'fellowship' is really disobedience to the Lord. The result is that there is almost no emphasis on evangelism in these churches."

This comment really made the Bethany Church board members squirm. They recognized that it was all too true of their church, but Rick bravely soldiered on to his next point.

"This next reason for decline probably doesn't characterize Bethany Church all that much," Rick began. "But you need to be aware of it. This may come to be a concern in this church if you are not vigilant on this matter. In some churches worship is elevated to the point that it subtly becomes an end in itself. Soon it isn't really about worshiping God. It is about getting the emotional high that comes from a great worship band, enthusiastic singing, and the freedom to raise one's hands and even dance around a little by your chair. Selfishness begins to intrude. Worship can become all about making myself feel good, feel connected, even feel "spiritual," but it really isn't about submitting to God and obeying him. And as Satan loves to do, he soon makes it the most important thing about church for a whole lot of people. But," Rick reminded them, "real worship is built on a rock solid commitment to obeying the Lord in all he has called us to do. If worship is taking place in a general atmosphere of disobedience to the Lord's command to make disciples of as many people as we possibly can, it really isn't worship at all. It can be a whole bunch of people getting all emotionally charged up as they sing their hearts out. But it really has a lot more in common with attending a rock concert than genuine worship. Real worship starts with obedience to the Lord. Until our churches are doing a bang up job of reaching lost people, there is a whole lot of false worship taking place."

Rick could get really exercised on this point. He had just had enough of believers who thought they were doing the will of God while they were refusing to get busy fulfilling the Great Commission. Until there were large numbers of people coming to faith in Jesus, Rick knew that there wasn't a whole lot of genuine worship taking place in his churches.

"I'll bet that as I teach on this seventh reason you will be able to think of some churches and maybe even some people in Bethany Church who fit this bill," Rick said as he began to explain the holiness approach. "These people equate holiness with following a very strict set of rules. These rules are not necessarily from the Bible. They are made on the basis of what some people believe to be some principle of Scripture. These people get to the point that they seem to think that if you are really holy, you will be really different.

"But in reality this is just one more way that Satan substitutes a phony for the real thing," Rick explained. "These people are guilty of adding to the Scriptures. It isn't enough to just follow the clear commands of Scripture. They go beyond, often way beyond, what the Bible requires of followers of Jesus. The sad part is that they impose their own standards on all other Christians and expect compliance with their rules. Anyone who fails to live up to their rigid regulations is not considered to be spiritual. Often the man-made rules they impose make them different from people around them in some really weird ways, ways not demanded by God.

"When that happens, it greatly hinders the effective spread of the gospel. When the gospel is presented it is understood that if one is to accept Christ he will also have to accept this lifestyle. Not surprisingly, people stay away from the gospel in droves when it comes in such a weird wrapper. Another thing that is so harmful about this approach is that it causes division between sincere fellow believers on matters that we have no business dividing over. And, lastly, these people get so wrapped up in formulating their rules and enforcing them on others that they lose interest in evangelism. They just don't have the time, energy, or even interest for things that don't further their personal version of Christianity."

Several of the board members nodded thoughtfully as they recognized this tendency in even some folks at Bethany Church. They were starting to understand that this wasn't just a harmless little obsession on the part of people who tended to these extremes. It was a real reason some churches were not reaching lost people and were not growing. They were seeing the common thread of self-obsession that characterizes all of these excuses for not reaching others.

"Okay, don't jump all over me quite yet," Rick said as he put the eighth point up on the screen. "Hear me out on this before you leap to conclusions. I am not in any way downplaying the importance of reaching lost people in other countries. We all know that this is part of obeying the Great Commission. What I am talking about is a church that is no longer maintaining a healthy balance between reaching people in other countries and reaching people in their own community."

Rick could see a few of the board members sitting back in their chairs after almost levitating when they first saw this point. Their body language told Rick loud and clear that they had been ready to say, "Okay, buddy. You've gone too far now!"

He went on to explain that this type of church was so committed to reaching people overseas that they forgot to commit the resources, energy, and sacrifices needed to reach their own area. He pointed out that often these churches were very proud of their missions program. They made it clearly the highest priority of the church. It is good to be committed to reaching other lands. There is nothing wrong with that at all. In fact, there is a whole lot that's right about it. The problem came in when this emphasis displaced any and all concern for the lost in the local community. Few resources of time, programming, staff, and money were earmarked for local outreach.

This was wrong for two reasons. One is that it was disobedience to the Great Commission. The second was a very practical reason. No church can long survive if the people are not reproducing themselves spiritually in their home town. "It's very simple," Rick said. "If you don't win the people around you, who will be the next generation in the church? But it is amazing, isn't it, that we can get so out of balance on this subject that we put the future of the "sending church" in jeopardy? One reason this happens is that it is so much easier to send money to support those who reach lost people in foreign countries than it is to actually share the gospel in your own town. Satan, once again, deceives us into thinking we are doing the will of God when we are really just being selfish. We are giving in to our fears, our laziness, and our desire to stay comfortable.

"That is the real reason churches with this approach end up dying," Rick expressed to the people in the room. He could see that they were getting the point. The question that remained was whether they would take any action in response to new information.

Rick felt strongly about communicating his next reason for church decline. He had, himself, been led to faith in Jesus by a staff member of a para-church organization. He had learned much from this organization as a university student. His life had been blessed by this group, and he deeply respected what they were doing. But he had also understood while he was involved with them, that while they enhanced the ministry of the local church, the local church was the center of what God was doing in the world. He knew that Christianity would rise or fall, not so much based on the success of para-church organizations but based on the success of the local church. He believed strongly that local churches should support and encourage the work of these ministry groups, but not at the expense of their own ministry and outreach to their community. He had seen churches that got out of balance on this. They became so enthusiastic about supporting para-church ministries that they neglected to reach out to the area around the local church.

Rick knew that this was really just a variant on the Foreign Missions Concentration. It was a way to avoid actually doing the work of evangelism oneself. It was a whole lot easier to pay someone else to do the evangelism. This emphasis became a way to avoid the responsibility that the people of the local church had, which is to reach lost people themselves. It was another way that Satan pulled his old trick of substituting something good for the best. It was also another way that people acted selfishly. In order to stay safe, comfortable, and risk-free, people would gladly pay someone else to do the evangelism for them. Rick just shook his head in front of these board members as he thought about how clever Satan is at disguising his real motive. His real motive was to make local churches completely ineffective at reaching their own community. This was just one more way he succeeded in his desire.

Rick was wondering if these board members could take any more today, but they seemed to be staying with him so he continued to the tenth reason for church decline.

"This is a condition in which church members place a higher priority on hanging together with their friends rather than reaching out to people who are slightly different than themselves," Rick began. "You remember not too long ago when the Swedish heritage in this church was so strong that anyone not Swedish by background was treated almost like an outsider? Well, that same kind of thing goes on today, only the distinguishing characteristics have changed with the generations. Now the ethnic background thing has changed to those who are more recent immigrants. Sometimes it has nothing to do with one's ethnic background at all. Sometimes it is just a cultural or style issue that has nothing to do with one's country of origin."

Rick proceeded to show them that when they made their own particular culture or style of a higher value than reaching lost people, it made them ineffective in obeying the Lord in this matter. It came down, once again, to giving in to their fears of people or cultures that were different, and choosing to stay in their own safe little world. That attitude hardly characterized the church of the first century, and in the isolated cases where it did show up, the Lord took definite action to get the people out of their comfort zone.

Rick knew that the same motivations are still as prevalent today as they were one hundred or even fifty years ago. The circumstances change, but the basic desire to avoid risk, stay safe, and live in the comfort zone of people like ourselves still hinders churches from reaching people for Christ.

"Folks, what happened to Jesus' statement that 'perfect love casts out fear'?" Rick asked. "When we rely on God's love, when we dwell in the knowledge that his perfect love will never let us down, our fears of boldly sharing the gospel with people unlike ourselves are taken care of.

"Really," Rick continued, "it isn't even so much a matter of people's fear of communicating with people unlike themselves. It is all about our desire to take the easy way out, to stay safe, to not take risks, and to focus on what we find pleasant, not what we find difficult. Jesus taught us that if we try to save our life, we end up losing it. If we lose our life for his sake, we find it. But that flies in the face of our human instincts to cling to our life for all we are worth. He calls us to trust him, not our human instincts. They are not reliable. Now, I would like to encourage each one of you here today to think of ways in which you are clinging to that which is safe, rather than risk reaching other people. And I would like you to think of ways in which Bethany Church as a group is guilty of living in your own cultural ghetto instead of reaching out to people outside the church."

Rick knew that this, his eleventh reason for church decline, was probably the greatest way in which Bethany Church was hindering its effectiveness in outreach. Rick knew that this could be a real sore spot for churches that valued their tradition over their effectiveness in outreach.

"I'd like you to really let yourself imagine how awkward and uncomfortable you would feel the first time you visited an Amish church service," Rick began. "Of course you would have to hitch a horse to a buggy, make your way down a road shared with cars, wear the black clothes, the bonnet and a long dress if you were a woman, and a long beard if you were a man. You would have no idea of what to do or when to do it in the service. The silences would make you uncomfortable, and you would be wondering if you would be expected to say something. The songs sung with no instruments would be totally foreign to you, and even the lingo they used would be hard for you to understand. Now I want you to also honestly try to imagine what it would be like for someone who has never been in church to come to one of your Sunday services. How comfortable would they feel with the way you dress, the type of music you use, and the 'insider language' floating around? Would they be feeling really awkward with silences in the service? Are there things in your service that would be totally unfamiliar to them? Would it seem to them that they had landed in another culture? Would there be any programs that were addressed to things they are concerned about or interested in?"

Rick went on to remind them that one of the most basic principles of missionary outreach is that the missionary must adapt himself or herself to the culture of the people they were trying to reach with the gospel. The missionary can't compromise on anything the Bible clearly commands or prohibits, but in all the spiritually or morally neutral ways possible, the missionary tries to be like the people he is reaching out to.

Rick brought to their attention just how much Christians are living in a culture that is foreign to them. "In order to reach the people in that culture, Christians have to be relevant to that culture," Rick said. "That desire to be relevant shows up in using a musical style familiar to the unbeliever, dressing in a way that doesn't make the unreached person uncomfortable, and preaching and programming in a way to bring the word of God to bear on the real concerns and problems of the un-churched person. These issues change in a culture with every generation. The church must be prepared, and even eager, to adapt their style to fit the new generation that is coming along." Rick could see the wheels spinning in the minds of each of the board members. They seemed to be getting the point.

"To reach people in another culture, we have to adapt to their style in all the ways that don't violate our spiritual and moral values."

Rick hoped that the members of this board would be able to share these insights with the congregation in a clear and convincing way. It was time for Bethany Church to ramp up its effectiveness in outreach.

"Is style of worship an essential of the Christian faith?" Rick launched into his twelfth point. "How about style of preaching or whether the Apostle's Creed is recited in the worship service? How about the kind of clothes that are worn to church? Or what form of education we decide to have our children involved in? Are any of these things essentials of the Christian faith?" Rick wanted to make them really think about these things. "Okay, are we all agreed that these are not essentials of the faith? But how many times have you found Christians arguing over this kind of thing? And, sometimes, these arguments get really serious. The people on different sides of these issues draw blood, so to speak. We are willing to write off Christian brothers and sisters over these things even though they are not essential to our faith. Can you see how this is a hindrance to obedience to the Great Commission?"

Rick went on. He forcefully opened their eyes to the fact that arguing over non-essentials is a tragic waste of our opportunity to be ambassadors for Jesus.

"First of all, people who are willing to draw battle lines over these minor issues are off track, they are not focused on outreach. They are expending their energies on things that don't really matter all that much instead of on the most essential matters. Second, the reputation of all Christians takes a hit when any of us behave in this way. The people around us are rightly disgusted by this kind of internal squabbling. Third, when we insist on maintaining non-essential beliefs and practices, we end up putting an unnecessary burden on anyone who wants to accept Christ. We require of them that they conform to our practices in these matters when the Lord doesn't require them to do this. It puts another barrier in the way of a person committing their life to the Lord. We want to remove barriers, not erect them."

Rick could tell that the people around the table with him were in agreement. He could also see that they were wrestling with the application of the point. What did this mean for them in real practical terms? What might they have to change in terms of what they regarded as essential and not essential to their faith?

"How attached are you to this building we are now sitting in?" Rick prodded them one more time. "If, starting next Sunday, you had to meet somewhere else, how would that make you feel? Do you believe that everything the Lord has called you to do could be done just as well in another building? What if you even had to start meeting in a school, or a community center building? Would all of that feel really painful to you? Would the worship of God be just as real in a school or community center building?"

Rick was trying to get them to think about his thirteenth and last reason for churches dying. He knew that far too many churches were being hindered by their building and its location. But because of an unwarranted level of reverence for the building itself, these churches were unwilling to change locations to enable themselves to become more effective in their service to the Lord and to the community.

He knew that Bethany Church would have this issue sometime in the next fifteen years, and he wanted them to start thinking about it now instead of waiting until it was too late. He didn't want them waiting until the church had shrunk to the point that it no longer had the resources to do anything about the problems the building presented. Rick tried to help them understand that so many Christians develop such strong emotional ties to the building itself that they stop thinking of the building as just a tool, and nothing more than a tool. To them the building becomes a "sacred place" in itself, a shrine. And when that building is no longer an effective tool, they cling to it for emotional reasons. They refuse to acknowledge that a change needs to be made.

"The church is not a building. It is a group of people who meet somewhere in a building. As long as that building remains an effective tool they should use it. But when it no longer is an effective tool, when it is about as ineffective as a hammer with a broken handle, it needs to be replaced with a tool better suited to the purpose at hand," Rick exhorted his listeners.

Some of the board members' eyes got a little wider as they started to get the drift of what Rick was really saying to them. Maybe they would have to start considering this with regard to the future of Bethany Church.

When Rick shut down the PowerPoint presentation and suggested that they take a fifteen-minute break, he could tell these people responsible for Bethany Church's future were ready for some relaxation. This had been a pretty heavy presentation for them to deal with. It had rattled some of their thinking and some of them seemed like they just wanted to think about something else for a while. Rick knew it would take some time for them to absorb all that he had shared with them, and he began to think through how he could lead them to make this something more than just an academic exercise. How could he lead them to actually do something about the parts of this that most applied to them? He wasn't sure yet just how to do that. After a time of discussion that really didn't get too involved, Rick said good-bye to each person in the room.

He reassured them that he was available to the group or to anyone individually to help them process the content of their time together. The group seemed pretty subdued. They were not resistant to what he had shared with them; they just seemed a little overwhelmed by it. Rick was not surprised with that outcome. He knew it would take some time for all this to sink in and for them to begin to formulate strategies based on this information.

Rick made a point of getting together with Al and Wayne as soon after this meeting as he could. He filled them in on all that had happened at Bethany Church. All three agreed that this had gone about as well as could be expected. It would take time for people to get their heads and hearts around these ideas, decide which of them applied most to them, and then take some action. All three thought Rick should continue to accept opportunities to teach these ideas and that they would each try to stimulate similar opportunities in their own regions. They spent time together praying fervently that the Lord would use what they were doing to activate the church and that he would guide them as to what they should do next.

Over the next year, Rick had a surprising number of opportunities to take leadership groups through this material. The highlight of the year was when the leaders of the region-wide men's retreat invited him to share this information. It was very well received, although some of the men, especially the older men, seemed scared by what the implications were going to be for their congregations. Rick's regional board decided that he should take several hours at the next regional conference to share these insights with all the lay delegates to the conference. Rick knew that this would be a real test of how well this information would be received, and he was both excited and apprehensive as he prepared to present to the largest group yet.

Both Al and Wayne were getting similar results in their regions. The excitement was gradually building in each of these regions. In spite of the fact that these principles were, to some degree, upsetting the apple cart of the status quo in the churches, people were listening very intently to what was being said. There was some resistance as these men pushed individuals and church boards out of their comfort zones. Many of the people realized on a deep, sometimes subconscious, level that something had to be done. They were tired of seeing churches decline and even close. They wanted some solutions even if it meant discomfort for themselves.

Things went well when Rick taught these things to the regional conference. Oh, there were a few people who grumbled about the fact that they thought he was being critical of them and their churches. And, in a way, he was! But Rick had learned how to be a gentle communicator on sensitive matters like this. He made sure to express his appreciation for all the years of hard work these people had put into keeping their churches afloat. Some of them had made heroic efforts to keep some of these churches alive and functioning. They just didn't understand that it was an impossible task unless some core issues were addressed. Rick gently addressed those issues and helped the people see that, with some changes, there could be hope again. For the most part the people were accepting of what he was teaching. Some walked away angry, but they were a small minority. Al and Wayne reported similar results in the opportunities they were having. Some of the other regional superintendents wondered why these three were stirring up so much trouble, especially the older superintendents who had made peace with the way things were. They weren't sure they wanted these young bucks getting people's hopes up, only to not be able to provide any solutions.

QUESTIONS FOR REFLECTION

1. In your estimation, how would your church react to straight talk concerning its present condition?

2. How would you describe the present condition of your church?

WHAT DO WE DO NEXT?

AFTER A SOLID YEAR AND A HALF OF TEACHING THIS MATERIAL IN AS MANY CHURCHES AND CONFERENCES AS THEY POSSIBLY COULD, RICK, WAYNE, AND AL GOT TOGETHER FOR A DOWNLOAD SESSION. What had they learned in this process? Were they any more hopeful about the future of these churches? It was clear to each of them that what they were teaching churches and leaders was getting through. People were taking seriously the information they were presenting. In a few cases, pastors and board members were starting to identify that some of these thirteen reasons for the decline of churches explained what had been happening in their ministry that they hadn't been able to identify. Something good was coming about from all their prayers, research, and hard work.

But the thing that was unsettling to them was that while people were starting to realize why churches decline, so far, however, no churches had been able to translate this knowledge into a turnaround. Even though some of these leaders had been able to pinpoint reasons for the decline of their church, none of them had, as of yet, been able to take the next step to producing growth in their churches.

"You know, guys," Al said to his two cohorts, "some of the

responsibility for this falls on our shoulders. We have gotten these leaders to recognize the problem, but they seem incapable of coming up with the solution on their own. Should we be surprised? I'm not sure that we have even developed the solutions to how to actually turn these churches around. We'd better be praying about this and trying to figure out how to coach churches to take the next steps."

This was a sobering realization for these three men. They had succeeded in creating understanding of the problems. Now they needed to be able to understand how to change the situation so they could lead pastors and churches to make these changes.

Over the next six months, Al, Rick, and Wayne prayed regularly for the Lord's guidance in finding solutions. They chatted on the phone or through e-mail whenever they could, but they were busy guys. They continued to teach the reasons for the decline of churches whenever they got the opportunity, with the same encouraging results. That actually made them feel more pressure to come up with solutions to the problem, not just an understanding of the problem. They really looked forward to the next time they could spend some concentrated time together to attack the solutions. That time came during the week between Christmas and New Year's Day. By then, they all needed a little respite from the busy schedule since Thanksgiving Day. They got together at Wayne's house for a whole day during that slow week after Christmas.

"Okay, guys, what has the Lord been showing you about how to turn these churches around?" was the first comment out of Wayne's mouth. Well, that was the first comment after the usual time of ribbing each other about the extra Christmas pounds they had each stacked on in the last month. They also took some time to pray for Al's son, Matt, who, as yet, had not shown any indications of growing any closer to the Lord. But then they got down to business.

It took almost a whole day of intense discussion and prayer to hammer out what they came to regard as the seven essential things churches were going to have to do and experience if they were going to turn around. They concluded that it was time for them to start teaching these principles to the churches they had led through the process of identifying the reasons for their decline. They also realized that these were so important and serious that it would be impossible to teach all seven of these principles at one time, unless it was in a week-long retreat setting. They began to pray together that the Lord would open up opportunities to begin teaching what they believed could turn churches from decline to growth. More importantly than just growth, their prayer was that this growth would come about because un-churched people would start coming to faith in Jesus.

On Monday morning as Rick got up from his knees in prayer, his office phone rang. He had been praying that the Lord would open an opportunity to share the new information the three had concluded would re-awaken dying churches. On the phone was the pastor of Bethany Church. Rick could tell he was a little irritated with Rick.

"Rick, you told us what was wrong with our church, but you haven't given us any help in solving the problems. This is really getting frustrating. We want to make things better, but we don't know how! Can you help us?"

"Yes," Rick replied. "I think I can help. This will probably take several sessions, but I believe I have information that I can share with you to help you make a fresh start. When can we set up a time for me to meet with you and the board at Bethany?"

"You know, I think I'd like to meet with you first by myself. The last time you were here you kind of stirred things up pretty good. I would like to have an idea of what you are going to bring to us this time before you drop the bomb on the board. When can we get together?"

He and Rick set a time the next morning to meet at the local IHOP over breakfast. When Rick laid out what he intended to talk about, the pastor was reassured and wanted to proceed with getting this teaching done with his board. They set up a time the next month when the pastor could pull the whole board together to try to take this thing the next step.

QUESTIONS FOR REFLECTION

1. Based on the information in this book, what do you believe it would take for your church to turn around?

2. How effective is your church in reaching un-churched people?

WEEK FOUR
STUDY GUIDE

1. Have the study group discuss the question, "Are there things that our church is clinging to that are not essential, and may even be hindering our effectiveness in reaching others?"

2. Have the group break up into groups of three or four people and identify the parts of our history that are helpful to celebrate and what parts we are holding to even though they are preventing us from being all that the Lord wants us to be today?

3. Break the group into two groups and have each of them design and present a simple drama of how they think the board of our church would react to the kind of teaching Rick was presenting to the board at Bethany Church.

WEEK FIVE

EVANGELISM

WHEN THE DAY ARRIVED TO MEET WITH THEM, RICK WAS GRATEFUL AND RELIEVED THAT FINALLY HE HAD SOMETHING CONCRETE TO GIVE TO THESE PEOPLE THAT SHOULD ENABLE THEM TO START THE CHURCH ON A NEW PATH. He greeted each person warmly as they came into the room. They seemed genuinely relieved to be able to start doing something positive about what they had clearly identified as their problems. They also seemed a little wary, hoping that Rick's teaching wouldn't just lead to more negative self-evaluation. They had already done enough of that. They wanted to get going in a positive direction and hoped Rick could help.

"Well, thank you all for coming out once again. After last time, I wasn't sure I would be invited back! I know that our last session wasn't easy for you. I know it led you to do some serious and difficult soul searching about why Bethany Church has been in decline for so long. Thank you for hearing me out and for doing the hard work of identifying several of the problems here at this church. My prayer is that today we can start in a positive direction. I pray we can find some ways to reverse the downward trend in this congregation. Please join me in prayer that God would himself lead this meeting, and that we would sense the Lord showing us a new way to life and health for Bethany."

Rick asked several of the board members to pray and concluded their time in prayer with these words, "Lord, we are your servants. We worship you today as the sovereign ruler of the universe. We know you are much more deeply interested in and committed to the future of Bethany Church than we are. Lord, show us the way. We desperately want this congregation to become a lighthouse for you in this community. We thank you in advance, Lord, for all the people who are going to come to believe in Jesus as a result of the changes this congregation is going to be making. We rejoice in your goodness and the assurance that you are here with us. We are not alone. You have promised to guide us if we do not stubbornly insist on our own way. We pray in the name of Jesus, your precious Son, our Savior. Amen."

"Dear, friends," Rick began, "Al Jones, Wayne Walczek, and I have been praying, literally, for several years about the condition of the churches in our regions. We have been beseeching the Lord to show us how to help churches that are at a plateau or are declining. We want so much to see churches filling up with new life and enthusiasm. We believe the Lord has led us to seven practices that churches will need to put in place in order to become dynamic growing congregations. I don't think we can cover all of this today, but let's do what we can and schedule a time later to finish this off. Shall we get started?"

"Yes!"

"Go for it!"

"What are we waiting for?"

"Before I get started on this first practice, I want to give one very important reminder," Rick said. "I know you all know this, but we all sometimes need a reminder. Here it is. The church doesn't belong to us! We all use the expression 'my church' and that's okay so long as we remember that the church belongs to him who gave his life to redeem it. We tend to get very possessive about the church. Soon we start thinking that since it is 'my church' it should do my will and serve my interests. Wrong! The church exists to do the will of God, not our will. Let us always keep that thought foremost in our thinking as we wrestle with how to make things better.

"Now, here is the first practice we must put in place to start reaching lost people and really growing. It will probably be the hardest practice to implement, but without it being fully implemented, nothing else is going to work right. We will be just spinning our wheels in frustration. Are you ready for it?" Rick asked.

"Yes!" The board members loudly replied. It seemed like their frustration was already starting to show.

"Okay, here it is then. For any church to be in a place of obedience to the Lord and for any church to begin to grow significantly, evangelism must become the number one priority. I understand that we must also do worship, discipling (teaching), and fellowship to be fully obedient to the Lord. But it only stands to reason that evangelism must be the first activity of the church. Unless people are won to faith in Jesus, there won't be anyone to worship, no one to teach, and no believers to fellowship with. If any church fails to win its generation to Christ, there will be no church in the next generation. In chronological order, evangelism must occur first so the other activities will have people to do them. And, remember something, all these other activities we can do in heaven. Worship will be perfectly genuine and wonderful to experience in heaven. We will never stop learning in heaven, and our minds will not be cluttered up with all the junk of the world, the flesh, and the devil to hinder our learning. And our fellowship in heaven will be perfect with none of the human selfish traits that ruin fellowship. The only one of these things we can't do in heaven is evangelism. That is the primary reason the Lord left us here on earth after we came to faith in Jesus. His primary command for the church until he returns is to make disciples of as many people as we possibly can during our lifetime on earth.

"Surely that makes sense to everyone here?" Rick asked rhetorically. While he asked the question rhetorically, the people in the room answered with an emphatic "Yes!"

"Okay, now I know you understand this in an intellectual sense," Rick responded. "But have you really thought about what that means in practice at Bethany Church on an everyday basis? Since 91 percent of American Christians now believe the church exists to take care of them and their families, it will require a massive re-orientation in people's thinking to get the priorities at Bethany Church straightened out. You can count on resistance to this change. Our culture has become very self-oriented, and this has penetrated the church rather thoroughly. People will probably fight ferociously against this change. Churches have split over this difference, and many pastors have lost their jobs for pushing a church to give up its pre-occupation with pleasing the members who are already there instead of reaching more people. When a pastor starts promoting this new agenda, some people will grumble that he doesn't care about them anymore. 'All he cares about is those other people' will be the accusation against the pastor.

"But, this is really quite ridiculous," Rick said rather forcefully. "Why would people think that a pastor who has a passion for reaching lost people would find it impossible to care about the people who are already in the church? They are acting like jealous little kids who cry as soon as Mama pays any attention to any other child! Let me use an illustration to explain this."

"Most Christians today seem to have the unspoken expectation that when they accepted Christ they signed up for a trip on a luxury cruise ship. On a cruise ship people are pampered, entertained, fed exotic foods and desserts, and have their every whim for pleasure and comfort satisfied. I don't know if you have ever noticed, but people who have gone on those trips usually come home grumpy and unhappy. It's easy to understand why. They have tried to find happiness by grasping for all the pleasure and comfort they can get. No one ever gets happy pursuing pleasure. That quest leaves people empty and frustrated instead of happy! Jesus said the only way to experience fullness of joy is to live in obedience to him. It's amazing to see how many Christians are still trying to find happiness by pursuing pleasure, comfort, and safety.

"What actually is true is that when a person accepts Christ as their Savior they sign up for a lifelong tour of duty on a warship. We must work together to fight a common enemy. We must enter the battle for the souls of lost people. Jesus has promised in Matthew 16:18, 'I will build my church and the gates of Hades will not overcome it.' What he is actually saying is that the gates of hell will not be able to resist the onslaught of the church. When we commit ourselves to the God-given task of reaching lost people, live in close fellowship with the Lord, and get busy sharing the gospel, Jesus' promise to build his church will be fulfilled. We will succeed in battering down the doors of hell and releasing people who are now held captive by the devil, the world, and the flesh.

"Now, are the people on a warship in times of war taken care of? Of course they are. They may not be fed exotic foods and desserts, but they are fed nutritious food that will make them strong in preparation for battle. There won't be a whole lot of emphasis placed on entertaining the troops will there? Instead the emphasis will be on training them for battle, preparing them to win at war. They will learn the tactics of the enemy. They will study how to defeat the enemy. And, they will drill their bodies so that they are in tip-top fighting condition. But are they being taken care of? Certainly they are! If they suffer a wound in battle, the medics will swarm around them to bind up their wounds and get them well again. All of this is done with the single goal in mind of winning the war, winning the individual battle we are engaging in for this day. People on warships receive excellent care! But it is a very different care than what one receives on a cruise ship!"

Rick almost shouted this point. He was really getting warmed up on this subject. He had endured so much frustration on this matter.

"People receive excellent care on a warship, but it has one end in mind. The purpose of this care is to prepare the people on that warship to win in battle. This care is not designed to give them a lot of comfort, pleasure, and safety. It isn't designed to pump up their egos. It is designed to prepare them to win in war! The problem is that most Christians today are expecting the church to give them cruise ship care. That is why they are so unhappy. That kind of care never makes anyone happy for more than a very short time. But woe to the pastor who stops giving them cruise ship care and tries to start giving them warship care! He will very likely be forced to resign his position. Do you see why this will be such a difficult transition to make in Bethany Church?" Rick queried them. "You will need to protect your pastor from the sometimes vicious attacks he is likely to face. You, as a board, will need to stand shoulder to shoulder, presenting a united front in favor of this change. If, when the arrows start flying at the pastor, you defect and leave him standing there all alone, this attempt will fail. He will probably lose his position. Are you prepared for this kind of struggle?"

The pastor looked a little scared as he contemplated all that lay ahead, but different ones responded, "Yes. We are!"

"We can't keep doing what we are doing, or the church will simply disappear." "We will be closing the doors before long if we keep this up."

"This will be hard, but let's start doing it."

"Let's not be reckless in applying these truths, but let's apply them."

"We have to do something, and it is clear this is the biblical mandate."

"Okay. Let's take a fifteen-minute break and come back for some more," Rick encouraged them. Rick realized that his legs were pretty tired as he headed for the restroom, and he mentally planned on a big cup of coffee as soon as he got back in the room. He would need it. He was far from through with this subject.

"Okay, folks, this is probably going to be difficult," Rick began as he started out the next session. "But, remember, we are not alone. Over ninety percent of the churches in America are either going to have to go through this transition or close their doors. Other Christians in other churches are going to have to wrestle their way through this hard transition. We must remember to pray for them. What it amounts to is that we are going to have to go back to living like the Christians did in the first century. Nothing less will do. Those Christians faced great persecution for sharing their faith. Every time they spoke the gospel they ran the risk of beatings or being forced into the great arenas of the Roman Empire to fight hungry lions, angry bulls, or raging bears. They faced the real possibility of being burned at the stake. Many were just simply executed by the soldiers by sword or spear or beheading. Did this stop them from spreading the gospel? No. Instead they spread the gospel so enthusiastically and fearlessly that soon it had taken over the great Roman Empire, the most powerful nation known to man up to this point in history. It took over to such an extent that it was named the official religion of the Roman Empire. Remember, this was an empire in which, for many, the official religion was worship of the emperor as a deity. It took an incredibly great and powerful influence in that nation to be able to bring about such a transition. We who live today can hardly comprehend the power and rapidity with which the gospel spread in the first century. That is what we have to get back to again if we have any hope of not disappearing from our nation. We Christians have got to once again realize that we are put here for one main purpose.

As 2 Corinthians 5:20 says, 'We are therefore Christ's ambassadors, as though God were making his appeal through us. We implore you on Christ's behalf: Be reconciled to God.' Evangelism, the reaching of lost people with the gospel, has got to become more important than any other thing the church does. We need to do the other things, but they must become subservient to the cause of spreading the gospel throughout a nation that is becoming very anti-Christian.

"Now that sounds good in theory," Rick continued, "but what will that look like in actual practice? First, I am convinced that most churches, most Christians, will have to face the fact that we all are living in blatant disobedience to the central command Jesus gave the church during this time. Christians will never accept the changes that have to be made unless they recognize the need for those changes. Christians have become so complacent and consumer-oriented in their thinking about the church that until they confess the hardness of their hearts in this matter, they will never accept the necessary changes. Trying to make these changes without first leading them to repentance will just ignite a war in the congregation.

"Next, everything the church does has to be examined with this thought in mind. Every ministry, every church service, every activity must be put through the grid of assessing evangelistic effectiveness. Every ministry should be required to submit a plan of how they will reach out to un-churched people in the area around the church in the next year. If they can't come up with a plan, the leadership of that ministry will be replaced or the ministry itself will be terminated. There will simply be no room in the overall ministry of this church for ministries that do not contribute to the evangelistic purpose of the church.

"Yes, but there are some ministries that can't be expected to reach our community aren't there? Surely you can't expect the foreign missions team to be able to reach local people! How can they do that?" retorted the chairman of the missions board.

"Yes, we can," replied Rick.

"How can you expect that?" this board member indignantly responded. "They are focused on reaching people in other countries. How can they reach people here?"

"Here's how," replied Rick. "Do you ever take short term missions trips?"

"Yes, we go to Mexico every year to either build homes for people who can't afford them or build churches for struggling congregations. But what does that have to do with reaching people in our own town?" said the chairman of the missions board.

"It's simple, really," said Rick. "Can an unbeliever lay bricks or blocks? Can an unbeliever frame a house? Can they pour concrete or install wiring or place shingles on a roof? Of course they can! They don't have to know the Lord to do any of those things. I wouldn't want them teaching theology to Mexican pastors, but they can certainly do these other things. When you plan your next trip to Mexico have the team members invite their unsaved friends, relatives, neighbors, or work associates to come along. Many people want to do things to help those less fortunate. When they come along they will not only do the manual labor but they will be spending all that time with Christians. They will eat lunch together, travel together, sit in the evenings visiting, and sleep in the same area. Do you think it might be a natural occurrence to share the gospel with them in these conditions?"

"Hmm, I think you have a point there. I never thought about that possibility. You know, I think that might work. Wow, I can really see the possibilities in that!" was the reply of the Missions Committee Chairman. The light really seemed to be going on for him.

"Every ministry can think creatively like that," Rick pointed out. "If there is an open gym time for playing basketball, men should be encouraged to invite their un-churched friends to play. If there is a children's soccer program, make sure some of the adult leaders and coaches are people from outside of the church. When non-Christians are around Christians in that kind of setting, it starts the evangelism process rolling. Unless of course the Christians are being bad witnesses. That means no outbursts of temper and profanity on the basketball court, no whining and complaining about the church or the pastor, and no fighting among the Christians. We have to be a good witness when we have these opportunities. Every ministry, if the leaders will think creatively, will find a way to include those who don't know the Lord in their activities. The church needs to make very clear that this is an expectation, even a requirement, for every ministry in the church. When we do that we know the Lord will begin to produce results from all this activity."

You could almost see smoke rising from their heads as the people were rapidly processing this information and thinking of ways that the ministries they were involved in could reach out.

"The next part of this," continued Rick, "is that the church will have to develop excellent ministries geared precisely for people who are not yet church attendees. Stop and think real hard for a few minutes about what the genuine needs and interests of the un-churched person really are."

Everyone sat there waiting for him to say more.

"No. I mean right now. Take a piece of paper and just start brainstorming. What are the people who live in your neighborhood, your un-churched friends, your co-workers, really concerned about? What do they need help with? What are they interested in?"

Rick waited for about five minutes as the board members started shuffling in their seats and scratching their heads. Most of them had never given any thought to this matter. Five minutes later Rick said, "All right, let's see what you came up with. Just shout out your ideas. There are no dumb ideas. All of these thoughts can help us understand how to program for un-churched people. What are they interested in, and what do they need help with?"

After an awkward pause, Hank hesitantly spoke up, "Well, my neighbor really likes to go to Colorado Rockies baseball games."

"Anything else he likes or needs?" Rick asked.

"Well, he and his wife both have children from former marriages and are having a dickens of a time trying to blend those two families."

"Good thought" said Rick. "Somewhere around half of all children are living or have lived in blended families. That has got to be one of the toughest things anyone ever attempts to do, blending two families into one. So, ministries to blended families would meet a huge need in our community. Any others?" Rick encouraged.

"So many people have gone through a divorce, and we all know how tough it is to recover from that," said Jana.

"So, how can we help them?" Rick asked.

"Well, I know there are some excellent divorce recovery programs available to us. Should we start a divorce care ministry?" Jana thought out loud. "Will non-Christian people come to that kind of ministry?"

"Excellent idea. Yes, if we invite them they will come. Any other ideas?"

"In these tough economic times, I feel so sorry for those couples who just can't seem to manage their finances. They are always living on the edge of bankruptcy. Plenty of them have already lost their homes to foreclosure," said Phil. "How can we help them?"

"There are some excellent programs designed to help people with their personal financial management that we can easily access. I know for a fact that some of them are very careful to make sure that they present the gospel in the course of their seminars. Why don't you start doing one of those ministries and invite people who don't attend church to come?" Rick suggested.

"Well, I don't know if this qualifies. It seems a little lightweight compared to these last three, but there are quite a few people, myself included, who are quite fascinated with the new digital photography and Photoshop software. Do you suppose a photography club would work?" Cindy asked.

"Why not?" Rick said. "Anything that is of help or interest to people who don't attend church can qualify for this type of program. You would want to make sure that the club had both un-churched people and people from your church attending. Rubbing shoulders with Christians over a period of time spanning several months is a tremendous first step toward accepting Christ. At least it is if the Christians are a good witness by their attitudes and their words.

"How about some major one-time events?" Rick pushed them farther. "Can you think of any that might attract people who don't know the Lord to the event?"

"I know of one very small church that puts on a fall party every year, and they have as many as seventeen hundred people attend that event. Surely we could do something like that couldn't we?" one of the members asked.

"You could, and you could try a community picnic in the park or a soccer tournament for children or a dramatic presentation at Christmas or Easter," encouraged Rick.

"Yeah. But I've seen churches do that kind of event quite successfully but no one ever seems to make the transition to attending church after the event", said Cindy. "That doesn't do a whole lot of good to put on a big event if no one comes to Christ and to church as a result of that event."

"That's right," Rick said. "These are some good ideas of one-time events. And you will be able to think of some events that are especially appropriate for your church. I encourage you to get creative in designing this type of event. But you're right. Unless careful thought is given to how to move people from that event to faith in Jesus and active church involvement, nothing much results. Let's take another short break; then we will jump into the next steps that are needed to bridge that gap."

People stood up stiffly and managed to get out the door of the meeting room. Rick could see this had been a long pull and was so grateful he hadn't tried to cover more subjects at one time. During the break he got a few of the guys to shoot some baskets for a few minutes to loosen them up and get their blood flowing again.

"Let's get going again," Rick said. "Two more main things to cover before we call it a day. Guys, I want you to remember back to when you were dating your wife. Of course you had to screw up your courage and ask her for that first date. Wasn't it exciting when she said yes she would be happy to have that date with you? Since you are now married, I assume that the first date went at least reasonably well. At least well enough that she accepted an invitation for a second date. Now how would that have worked if you had experienced a wonderful first date with her but never called her back again for a year and then asked her out for the same first date? Ladies, how would you have reacted if your husband had gone on a wonderful first date with you and not called you back for a year? What are the chances you would be married to him now?"

"No way!"

"That would so not happen!"

"Not a chance!"

"But," said Rick, "I see churches doing this kind of thing all the time. No wonder not many 'marriages' result from their activities.

"Churches should make sure that they don't just have great 'first dates' with un-churched people then have no contact with them for a year and then invite them to the same 'first date' activity. Churches need to carefully plan 'second date' and 'third date' activities to follow their big one-time event activities. Actually some of the ministries you mentioned earlier make up great second dates and third dates. Say you have a fall party that attracts five hundred or one thousand people. That constitutes a great first date. But how do you get to a second or third date? Carefully plan the second or third date activities even before you conduct the fall party. At the fall party hand out well designed and printed invite cards to things like parenting classes, personal financial management classes, or divorce recovery. Have multiple places at the fall party where these cards are being handed out. People will drop some of them and need more copies. They may even take some to invite their friends.

"Second dates work best if they are not one-time events. They work best if they are a series of weekly meetings on the given subject. Make sure there is a mix of church people and people who don't attend the church at these weekly meetings. Somewhere in the course of these meetings, at a natural point of insertion, make sure the gospel is clearly presented with an opportunity to respond in a more private way such as marking a card. If it works out, the gospel can even be presented several times in several different ways during these meetings. After hanging out with people from the church for a few weeks or months, some of the people in the second date activity will naturally want to try out a Sunday service. To help that process along, the church should plan third date activities.

"The ideal third date is a special Sunday morning service designed to complement the second date activity. If the second date is a series of classes on personal financial management, plan a Sunday service geared around celebrating financial freedom. The pastor can preach on the subject, testimonies could be given by some of the class participants, and certificates could be passed out. The congregation can cheer loudly for those who have completed the course. That accomplishes several objectives. First, it makes the class attendees feel welcomed and at home in the service. Second, it shows them that the church really is relevant to their lives. And, third, it encourages other people to attend the next section of the financial freedom course. Some un-churched people will follow the path of first, second, and third dates to accept Christ and become part of the bride of Christ, the church. But careful planning is required to make sure a logical progression such as this is available for numerous ministries and activities within the church. Is this starting to make sense to you all?" questioned Rick.

"Yes, this really makes sense," Cindy said. "Why don't more churches do this kind of thing? I believe it would solve the problem of people not coming back after the one-time events."

"I think the main reason churches don't do this careful planning is that they really aren't doing any careful planning with regard to outreach, period," Rick replied.

"There is one other important component to this that we should be sure to include," he continued. "Most of the people of our churches have no experience or training in how to be an ambassador for Christ. They are completely clueless about how to do this. They have been hiding in the closet so long they just don't know what to do. Trying to be 'God's Secret Agent' has become a lifelong habit for most of the people in our churches and will be very hard to break. We are commanded to be witnesses for our Lord. Where do we start getting people prepared to do that? Being a personal witness for the Lord is not complicated. It involves several very simple things. First, people have to be in relationship with those who don't know the Lord. Christians should deliberately cultivate relationships with friends, neighbors, relatives, and work associates who are not yet Christians. They should spend time with them doing things that are just fun things to do. Second, the Christian should identify that he is a Christian early in the relationship. You don't have to say, 'Hey. Did you know I'm a Christian?' like it is a dirty little secret. But talk about church activities. If they bring up a problem in their life, ask them if you can pray for them about it, and mention that the Bible says something about their concern. Show them that the Bible does actually speak to the concerns they have. Third, be genuinely helpful to them. Offer to do things like help them put the siding on their house or fix their car or babysit the kids for a few hours so they can go out on a date. Love them in real, practical, and helpful ways. Lastly, be prepared to share the words of the gospel with them when the opportunity arises. If nothing else, have a simple little booklet like 'The Bridge', put out by The Navigators available. Anyone can read one of these little tracts to your friend or neighbor, and it will do a great job of communicating the truths of the gospel. There are some really good study materials available on the subject of relational evangelism. I would encourage you to start using these materials in your small groups so that in a year's time each small group has gone through these materials. The pastor needs to continually keep before the people the awesome privilege we have in representing our beloved Savior to people who need to know him."

Rick wanted these people to realize that they had an opportunity to encourage all the people in the church to take their ambassadorship seriously.

"We don't have a choice about whether we are going to be Christ's ambassador," Rick said. "The only choice we really have is whether we are going to be a good ambassador, representing him well, or a poor ambassador who never speaks of his Master.

"All right, hang in there with me for a few more minutes. We have one more important subject to cover before we call it a day. That subject is the church budget."

Groans rose from the room. Clearly that was not their favorite subject, especially at the end of a long day.

"It will be all right." Rick tried to calm them down. "We aren't going to go into this in any great detail. We will cover this in general terms. I don't know how many of you have realized it, but the budget is really the church's plan for ministry covering the next year. For some churches this is the most concrete plan they will make for the year. Their budget decides for them what they will or will not do this year. If you want to find out if a church actually has a heart for reaching lost people, look carefully at their budget. How much money are they planning to spend on activities that have the hope of reaching out to people who are not yet part of the church? For most churches, that number is zero or mighty close to zero. If a church is unwilling to spend any money on outreach, how can they have any hope of bringing people to faith in Jesus? The budget needs to reflect a commitment to reaching the church's community with the gospel. Fortunately, most of the items contributing to outreach are not real big-ticket items. One-time events usually don't require thousands of dollars in the church budget. Second date and third date activities usually are not very costly. But there may be a few items that could be fairly costly. Developing a soccer field to host soccer leagues and tournaments may cost twenty thousand dollars, but it may be one of the most effective ways to reach a community that doesn't have youth sports activities put on by the city's recreation department. It will cost something to put on a first rate dramatic presentation. But if just a few families come to Christ, become members of the church, and are taught to become faithful tithers, that money will soon be coming back into the church coffers. Probably nothing the church spends money on has as great a hope of returning the investment quickly as do outreach expenditures.

"The church budget should show expenditures for outreach training materials, refreshments for outreach events, travel to outreach training seminars for church staff members, and expenditures for a church growth consultant," Rick continued. "Jesus himself said in Matthew 6:21, 'For where your treasure is, there will your heart be also.' When we invest money in something, we have a much higher interest in seeing that it succeeds. If we invest no or little money in outreach it is proof positive that our heart isn't in it. My prayer is that next year's budget for Bethany Church will reflect a real passion for reaching lost people.

"Well, that wraps up the content of what I wanted to communicate today. There is more to this that we will need to cover in future sessions, but I think we have put in a long day already. I won't start anything more today. Do you have any questions for today?"

"Yes, how do we get started?" asked the pastor. Rick could tell he was feeling a little overwhelmed by all this, and for good reason. This represented a major shift in the ministry of Bethany Church.

"Start by getting a good night of rest tonight and have a relaxing day tomorrow," Rick said. "I know you feel a little overwhelmed by all this. That's okay and even to be expected. Rome wasn't built in a day. This is a great change in the focus of Bethany Church. I wouldn't want you to charge out and try to get this all accomplished this week. Take some time. Be consistently praying about this together, asking the Lord to show you where to begin. I am available to you as quickly as a phone call or e-mail.

"In a couple of weeks, I will be back to teach more on the subject of awakening Bethany Church. There is more to it, but this is the most crucial part that we covered today. The Lord will guide you in this process. You can count on that. Be praying for receptivity on the part of the other members of the congregation. Be praying for wisdom about the sequence of steps required to get this started. The

Lord will make it clear, and I will help you every step of the way. I will see you again in two weeks. Until then, I will be praying for you also."

As Rick drove home that evening, he was exhausted.

This truly is spiritual warfare trying to revive dying churches, he thought. *I must make sure I have a team of people praying for me as I do even more of this work in the future. Satan will do everything in his bag of devious tricks to prevent the success of this effort.*

But Rick also felt a deep satisfaction. He knew this was about as devastating a blow as he could strike at Satan's kingdom. The Bible says in 1 John 3:8, "The reason the Son of God appeared was to destroy the devil's work." Rick was determined to further the work of our Lord. He felt like that day's meeting was the start of a strong attempt to destroy the devil's work. Rick knew that this was only the beginning, but it had been a good beginning. He would be with this group of leaders again in two weeks and looked forward to striking another telling blow at the enemy's stronghold. Later that evening Rick conferred with his three buddies in this endeavor via conference call. They all rejoiced with him that a good start had been made and agreed to pray for his next meeting at Bethany. They also requested his prayers that they would get some of these meetings set up in their own regions. All in all, Rick slept well that night, both from exhaustion and with the satisfaction that comes with accomplishment.

QUESTIONS FOR REFLECTION

1. In what ways is your church functioning like a "cruise ship" and in what ways as a "warship"?

2. In your community what ministries do you think would most meet the needs of un-churched people who are culturally like the people of the church?

WALKING BY FAITH

WHERE DID THOSE TWO WEEKS GO? Rick thought as he drove to Bethany Church for his next time of teaching. He was curious to see the emotional state of the members of the board of Bethany Church. Two weeks of reflection would have either given them enthusiasm and confidence to tackle this major undertaking or they would be filled with fear and hesitation at what lay before them.

As he drove the last five miles to the church, he prayed fervently that the Lord would work powerfully in that day's meeting and that he would have wisdom from above to lead this group in the right direction.

"Well, here we are again," Rick started, after having warmly greeted each person as they entered the room. "How are you all doing? Are you feeling overwhelmed by what we talked about last time, or are you encouraged to take on this major transformation of Bethany Church?"

Most of the people responded quite positively. A few were obviously willing but also just as obviously a little fearful of what lay ahead. Well, as Rick was about to share with them, a little fear was actually a good sign.

"Today we are going to meet head on with one of the scariest practices a church must develop if they are going to be powerfully used by God to reach a significant number of unreached people. If a church is going to see God at work in their midst, they must develop the practice of taking significant risks."

The response on the faces of the board members was immediate and negative. They, like most churches in America, had developed the philosophy that risk was a bad thing and that all risk must be avoided at all costs. They had come to think that risk taking was a mark of a "wild-eyed radical" who must be kept away from the church lest he damage the flock. They had come to value prudence as a virtue above most other character traits. Rick could see that he was going to have his hands full with this crew today.

"Ladies and gentlemen," Rick said, "I want you to think of the church of the first century. Was that church characterized by a desire to avoid all risk? Would their actions have been in keeping with our word *prudence*? Were they known for playing it safe?" There was a sort of reluctant, grumbling assent to the point Rick was making.

"Why would we think God would want us to live differently in our day? In fact, he wants us to live the way they lived, by faith. What does that mean? It is so far from the way we live that it is going to take some real searching of the Scriptures and of our hearts to bring the two of them into alignment with each other. Let's start with Hebrews 11:1, 'Now faith is being sure of what we hope for and certain of what we do not see.' In other words, living by faith means we live in the realm of that which we are not able to count, measure, see, or experience with any of our physical senses. Yet we believe that God will cause things to happen in that realm. We believe it because God has promised in Ephesians 3:20 to 'do immeasurably more than all we ask or imagine, according to his power that is at work within us.' We don't believe this because there is some human way to measure it. We believe it because we are trusting God to do what seems humanly impossible. Living this way is the only way to please God. Hebrews 11:6 says, 'Without faith it is impossible to please God, because anyone who comes to him must believe that he exists and that he rewards those who earnestly seek him.' Hebrews chapter eleven could very well be titled 'Faith's Hall of Fame' because it gives us example after example of people who lived by faith and pleased God. We will get back to some of those examples in a moment, but let's first consider some definitions.

"Second Corinthians 5:7 says, 'We live by faith, not by sight.'

In other words, the two are opposite of each other. We will live one way, or we will live the other. Walking by faith means believing God for what is beyond what we can see, touch, count, or measure. We see an example of this in Isaiah 31:1, 'Woe to those who go down to Egypt for help, who rely on horses, who trust in the multitude of their chariots and in the great strength of their horsemen, but do not look to the Holy One of Israel, or seek help from the Lord.' What is the context of this statement? The Israelites were facing a far superior enemy force. Instead of trusting the Lord to give them victory, no matter how strong the enemy forces, they relied only on human strength. They counted up the enemy's chariots, horsemen, and foot soldiers and said, 'Whoa, we can't fight these guys. They way outnumber us!' So they made an alliance with Egypt to fight for and with them. Of course they had to pay the Egyptians to do that. But, most importantly, they paid a price with God. He caused them to be soundly defeated even with the Egyptians' help. God wanted them to trust him to do that which was humanly impossible. He had done that for them over and over in the past, and he would have done it for them again if they had just trusted him. Do you see how being afraid to trust the Lord for that which is humanly impossible cheats us out of seeing God do remarkable things on our behalf?

"Churches don't count chariots and horsemen," continued Rick, "but what do they count?" The board members looked at him with blank stares. "Come on, guys. You can think of what we count," cajoled Rick. "Give me some ideas."

"Well maybe we do count chariots when we look at the parking lot, especially if we are noting the number of Mercedes compared to the number of old clunkers."

"We count dollars."

"We count numbers of people in the church for a given service."

"We count the number of workers for our various ministries."

"There is nothing wrong with counting those things," Rick assured them. "The only thing wrong is if we base our decisions only on the numbers without counting on God to do that which is beyond what the numbers tell us is possible.

"We see another example of this in 2 Chronicles 16:9, 'For the eyes of the Lord range throughout the earth to strengthen those whose hearts are fully committed to him. You have done a foolish thing, and from now on you will be at war.' Again, this is an example of the same things. The King of Israel, Baasha, set up a blockade around the people of Judah. God wanted them to trust him to give them victory supernaturally. Instead they paid money to the King of Aram to break his treaty with Baasha and come to their side. Politically it may have seemed like a wise thing to do. The problem was that it left God out of the picture. God wanted to give them a supernatural victory. Instead they put their trust in a human resource. God said to them, 'I am looking all through the earth for those who will trust in me to do the supernatural. When I find them I will strengthen them. Because you foolishly chose to trust in human strength rather than trusting in my supernatural power you will be at war from now on. You will not gain victory using the strategy of relying only on human resources.' Over and over again in the Scriptures we see that God wants to give supernatural victory and provision to those who will trust him to do what is humanly impossible. The problem is that we are unwilling to trust him to do anything beyond what we, by our own human resources, can do. Are you starting to see the necessity of walking by faith, not by sight?" Rick pressed them on this point.

"Let's look at one more example," said Rick. "We all know the story of David and Goliath, but have we really thought about what it teaches us about how we are to live? It shows us that faith can't just be in faith. Faith has to be in the proper object, namely, God and his promises. But, you say, what promise did David have to rely on when he confronted that gorilla Goliath? The promise of Genesis 15:18-21, 'On that day the Lord made a covenant with Abram and said, "To your descendants I give this land, from the river of Egypt to the great river, the Euphrates-the land of the Kenites, Kenizzites, Kadmonites, Hittites, Perizzites, Rephaites, Amorites, Canaanites..."' God promised Abram to give him the promised land. That land was inhabited by the Kenites, Kenizzites, and all those other ites. So God was promising that he would give victory over all the inhabitants of this land. When David walked up he discovered that the whole Israelite army was cowering in fear of the Philistine giant Goliath. Goliath daily taunted them. He declared that if any one of their soldiers would come out and defeat him man to man the whole Philistine army would surrender. Not one of the Israelite soldiers would accept his challenge. Not until David showed up on the scene.

David wasn't a soldier. He was taking care of his father's sheep and would occasionally be sent to bring some food to his three older brothers who were in the army. But David had a different response than all those other soldiers.

"When David walked up and saw Goliath and heard his taunts, he was ashamed and incensed that no Israelite soldier was willing to trust God enough to go fight Goliath. None were willing to trust in God's supernatural power instead of just their own. David had a different response in First Samuel 17:26, 'David asked the men standing near him, 'What will be done for the man who kills this Philistine and removes this disgrace from Israel? Who is this uncircumcised Philistine that he should defy the armies of the living God?' Notice his words, 'Who is this uncircumcised Philistine that he should defy the army of the living God?' The issue here for David was the honor of God's name. He knew that God would give supernatural power to win this battle if anyone would just trust God to do the supernatural. Of course Goliath was fearful. He was nine feet tall and heavily armed, but David didn't see Goliath's fearful stature. He saw only God's power and greatness. David refused to let the honor of God be taunted by a pagan giant. He sprang into action. Notice the words with which he addressed this giant in 1 Samuel 17:45-47:

> David said to the Philistine, "You come against me with sword and spear and javelin, but I come against you in the name of the LORD Almighty, the God of the armies of Israel, whom you have defied. This day the LORD will hand you over to me, and I'll strike you down and cut off your head. Today I will give the carcasses of the Philistine army to the birds of the air and the beasts of the earth, and the whole world will know that there is a God in Israel. All those gathered here will know that it is not by sword or spear that the LORD saves; for the battle is the LORD's, and he will give all of you into our hands."

"He walked up to this giant with only a sling and some small stones in his hands and in essence said, 'Goliath, prepare to die. I don't care how big and tough you are. I come in the name of the

Lord Almighty. He will give you over to me. I am going to cut off your head in just a few minutes here. Get ready to die! Not only that, but the whole Philistine army will be given into our hands.' Of course we all know what happened. We know the story well, but we refuse to learn its lessons and live according to them. We see example after example of the fact that God is just waiting for someone to trust him to do the supernatural. When we are willing to trust him to do far beyond what we can do for ourselves based on our own strength, resources, and wisdom, he springs into action. Only when we trust him to do the supernatural does he begin to act in powerful ways in our circumstances.

"Remember," said Rick, "genuine faith is always manifested in our actions. That is what James 2:17 is trying to get across when it says, 'In the same way, faith by itself, if it is not accompanied by action, is dead.' He isn't saying that we are saved by works. He is saying that genuine faith always manifests itself by taking action. If there is no action it proves we don't have faith. We call it 'stepping out in faith.' If David had just stayed in camp praying for the defeat of Goliath, nothing would have happened. Instead, David picked up his sling and stones and went toe to toe with Goliath, fully expecting that God was going to give him the victory. God acts after we take action. The Israelites had to actually step into the Jordan River before God parted the waters. They couldn't just stand on the banks praying that God would part the waters. He had already promised them he would, but he waited until they took action based on their faith in him. Remember something else: God often puts us into situations that are humanly impossible so that when we trust him and he saves the day, he gets all the glory. He also expects us to step into situations that are humanly impossible in faith that his power is sufficient.

"Let's look at one more example before we take a break," Rick said. "You probably remember the story of Gideon. It is recorded for us in Judges six and seven. Because the Israelites disobeyed the Lord and did evil in his sight, he gave them into the hands of the Midianites for seven years. Every year when the Israelites planted their crops, the Midianites came up with their herds of camels and camped on the land. They ruined the crops, and the Israelites had no food. The Israelites cried out to the Lord, and he raised up Gideon to lead them. Gideon wasn't exactly eager for the task, however. When the angel of the Lord said to him, 'The Lord is with you, mighty warrior,' he, after looking around to see who the angel was talking to, said, 'If the Lord is with us why has all this happened to us? The Lord has abandoned us into the hand of Midian.' The Lord said to him, 'Go in the strength you have and save Israel out of Midian's hand. Am I not sending you?' Gideon's response was something along the lines of 'Surely you jest! I am the weakest member of the weakest family in Israel, and you say that I am going to save Israel out of Midian's hand!?' The Lord gave him sign after sign that he would empower him for the task and finally Gideon agreed to go. He raised up an army of thirty-two thousand soldiers. The Lord said, 'That's too many men. Send all the ones who are afraid home.' Twenty-two thousand went home, leaving only ten thousand. I imagine Gideon became a little uncomfortable about then. But God kept at it saying, 'Still too many men. Take them to the water. Keep only the ones who lap with their hands instead of bending down with their mouths to the water.' Only three hundred men were left after this little test. With three hundred men, God gave Gideon and his men a supernatural victory. The Lord tells us what his motivation was for reducing the army to three hundred men in Judges 7:2, 'You have too many men for me to deliver Midian into their hands. In order that Israel may not boast against me that her own strength has saved her.' God knew that if thirty-two thousand men had gained the victory over the Midianites, they would have come back into town pounding their chests and singing 'We Are the Champions!' They would have boasted in their own strength. God wanted all to see that the victory was due to his power, and his alone. Are you starting to see a pattern here?

"God wants everyone to see and know that it is his power that is winning the day. He doesn't want anyone boasting in their own power, so he deliberately puts us into situations that are impossible for us to handle in our own strength. When we trust him and he gives a supernatural victory, then all the glory goes to him. Another example of that is when the Israelites had been delivered from Egypt. They were 'getting out of Dodge' so to speak and were well on their way to the promised land. They could have just gone around the end of the Red Sea and been on their way. But God said to Moses, 'I want you to go back and camp so the Israelites will be right between the Red Sea and Egypt. Pharaoh will see this and think that they are confused or lost. It will embolden him to try to get the Israelites back to be his slaves again. He will send his armies after the Israelites.' In Exodus fourteen, God explains his actions with these words, 'But I will gain glory for myself through Pharaoh and all his army, and the Egyptians will know that I am the LORD.' We all know the outcome of that one. The Lord parted the Red Sea so the Israelites could walk through it on dry land. He then brought the water crashing back over the Egyptian army so that all of them were drowned. Both the Egyptians and the Israelites knew that the Lord, and only the Lord, gave them the victory that day.

"But here is the point I really want you to see: God deliberately directed the Israelites to turn back so they would be trapped between the Red Sea and the Egyptian army. The Egyptian army was an overwhelming force. When the Israelites left Egypt there were six hundred thousand men plus women and children. Pharaoh sent six hundred of his best chariots to recapture the Israelites. Plus, he sent all his other chariots, plus horsemen, plus foot soldiers. Chariots were the tanks of the day. There were a huge number of chariots bearing down on the Israelites. And that was just the chariots. There were all the other horsemen and all the foot soldiers. The Israelites were not trained for war and had the most primitive of weapons. Do you think that was a slightly scary sight for the Israelites to see?" He paused as the board considered the scary position that God had put his people in. Then Rick said, "Okay, let's take a break, and I will summarize this when we get back."

After everyone had stretched, moved around, visited the restroom, and helped themselves to more goodies, Rick started again.

"Let me try to summarize the principles of walking by faith and then make some applications to our church situations. First, walking by faith means believing God for that which is beyond all our own human ability to accomplish. The situations that require walking by faith are humanly impossible situations. One way to say that is this: if we walk by faith we attempt something so great that unless God intervenes we are bound to fail. Second, it is *walking* by faith, not *sitting* by faith. Genuine faith always manifests itself in taking action. It isn't enough to say we trust God to do that which is humanly impossible. We also have to take action based on that faith. Faith in God releases his blessings, but we have to step out first. We can't just sit and wait for God to act. The Bible is full of all the ways he has already acted on our behalf. Now, he is waiting for us to act according to his promises and his nature. When we do, he begins to act on our behalf. We will not experience God's blessings unless we step out in faith.

"Third, faith must be in the proper object, God and his promises. It isn't enough to just have faith in faith. Some people seem to think that if they just have enough faith they can actually will things to happen and they will happen. But that isn't faith in God and his promises. That is faith in our own faith. The more we study the Bible, the more bold we become in trusting God for the humanly impossible because we learn more of the promises of God, and we see more examples of how God has worked on behalf of his people.

Fourth, God often deliberately leads us into situations that are, for us, impossible. These times can be very scary for us, but God does this so that we will learn to trust in his supernatural power and learn to take action based on his promises and his character as revealed in Scriptures.

"Now, let's make some applications to our own lives and to our churches," Rick continued. "As churches, we must, absolutely must, stop taking action only on the basis of what we can accomplish in our own strength, power, money, or resources. I can't tell you how many times I have seen churches approach budgeting by saying, 'How much did we bring in last year? We will budget based on the same amount of income this year.' They are not trusting God to do anything beyond what they themselves did last year. They look at last year's income and say, 'That's how much we can do this year.' There is not much thought given to what they should be doing. They let themselves be limited by what they think they can do with their own resources. Our first concern should not be whether something *can* be done. Our first concern should be whether something *should* be done. If God wants it to be done, we have to assume that he will provide the resources for it to be done. Here is another very important budgeting principle. If our budget does not reflect that we are trusting God to do that which is humanly impossible, it isn't a faith budget. There has to be the element of expecting God to do more than we can do ourselves.

"Not just in our budgeting, but in our programming decisions, there has to be evidence that we are expecting God to do more than we can possibly do ourselves. For example, we expect God to bring us more people. If we are serious about making evangelism the number one priority for our church, we have to expect that God will produce results from those efforts. Do you really think that if we set our hearts and actions to do the thing that is most important to the Lord, he won't produce results? That means we will have more people around here. That means we will have more children in the various aspects of our children's ministry. Therefore, we plan for more children than we currently have. That means we recruit more volunteer workers, we provide more space for children, and we hire more paid staff. Ah, that brings me to another point," Rick said. "I watch so many churches have the attitude that they will not hire additional staff until they have the money already saved up for their salary. Where is the faith in that? We always hired staff before we had the money in place to pay their salary. God expects us to walk by faith. But, on a more practical point, any staff hired to do direct people ministry will bring more people into church resulting in more money in the offering in a short period of time. If you hire a bookkeeper it probably won't have that same effect. But any program staff, if they are doing a good job, will result in more people in the church and more money in the offerings.

"Walking by faith means that we trust God to produce results from our efforts to reach people not currently attending church. That means we *expect* the church to grow. If we expect the church to grow, we will make plans to accommodate that growth. We will recognize that, for example, we might need ten more small groups by the end of this year. That means we will make sure our program of training small group leaders is functioning at a high level. It means we don't just sit and do nothing until there is a crisis because we have all these people who need to be in small groups, but we don't yet have leaders trained to lead small groups. Walking by faith requires us to be proactive, not just reactive. Being proactive means we plan as far ahead as we need to plan so that when God does produce results we are not caught off guard.

"This also shows up in our plans for facilities. We don't just base our facility plans on the number of people we currently have attending. We plan on the fact that the Lord is going to send us a whole lot more people than are currently here. So we buy enough land to accommodate significant amounts of growth. We master plan the whole site we own instead of just planning one building, constructing it, and then discovering later that it is going to be difficult to add to it and the result will look like the house that Jack built. Each step of construction is planned before we build any of the steps so that they all fit together when they are all done. How many times have I worked with churches where it is obvious that the people who built the first building had no vision beyond the congregation that existed at the time of construction? They bought one or two acres of land. They built one building that they clearly assumed was the last building they would construct, and as soon as they reached the capacity of that building they just shut down any more attempts to reach more people. They were already full, so why try to reach any more people? Never mind that they were situated in a city with hundreds of thousands of unreached people all around them. They were content with the congregation as it was, and they made no plans to reach any more people. Their lack of faith was clear for all to see. All you had to do was look at their building. Obviously they didn't expect the Lord to bring them any more people. Truth be known, they probably didn't even want the Lord to bring them any more people. If he did, it would disturb their comfortable little world.

"Walking by faith seems like a scary way to live, doesn't it? And if we look at it with the eyes of the flesh, it *is* a scary way to live. If we only see it in terms of what we can accomplish ourselves with our own resources, then of course it is scary to think about walking by faith. It means we actually have to place our trust in the Lord to do the impossible. It is always scary to trust someone other than ourselves. It is scary until we come to the realization of just how untrustworthy *we* are. When we come to realize that it is a whole lot safer to trust the Lord than to trust ourselves, then walking by faith is actually a great comfort. We don't have to trust in our own fallen nature, our own limited resources, or in our own clearly fallible wisdom. We can tap in to the supernatural supply of resources, wisdom, and power that the Lord makes available to us. That sure seems like a safer way to live to me. How about you all? Would you rather trust yourself or the Lord?", Rick needled these folks a little.

"Well, when you put it that way, of course I should feel safer trusting the Lord rather than myself," commented Cindy. "But it is hard to break those lifelong habits of trusting ourselves rather than trusting the Lord isn't it?"

"Oh, yes. It sure is," Rick responded. "That is why God deliberately puts us into humanly impossible situations, so that we see clearly what he will do on our behalf if we just trust him. We don't learn these lessons overnight. It is actually a lifetime of learning these things. But the more we learn to trust the Lord the more peace and contentment we gain in life and the less stress we create for ourselves.

"It is going to be hard work to get a congregation that has been accustomed to only walking by sight to start walking by faith. I hope you realize that," Rick said. "There will be significant amounts of resistance to this new way of doing things. Some people will probably leave the church. They are so convinced that caution is the godly way to live that they will never see the light. They will never realize that caution is not the way the Lord has called us to live. He has actually called us to live in a way completely opposite of that. He has called us to walk by faith, not by sight. You all will have to make sure that in your personal lives you are modeling walking by faith not by sight if you expect people to follow your leading the congregation to walk that way."

"What do you mean by that?" Hank asked.

"Well, let me give you just one example," Rick replied. "Are you already giving at least ten percent of your income to this congregation? If not, why not? Do you not trust that when you obey the Lord in this matter he will keep his promise to provide for you? You may think, 'Well my giving is my business and nobody else's.' And you may be able to keep this a secret in the sense that no one in the church, beyond the financial secretary, will actually see your giving record. But even if they don't know the actual numbers of your giving, it will show up in the way you approach the business of the church. If you are not obeying the Lord in your own giving, you will be very reluctant to have the church step out in faith in any financial way. You will not be able to keep your lack of faith a secret. Your attitude will betray your lack of faith. Titus 2:7 says, 'In everything set them an example by doing what is good.' You need to be an example to fellow believers in all things. This includes being an example of giving. The idea that our giving should be totally a secret precludes being an example in giving. You will also need to be an example of walking by faith with regard to being a witness. People will need to see that you have made a significant effort to be a bolder witness and stop being 'God's Secret Agent.' You may not be an expert personal witness yet, but you will have to let the congregation see that you are at least trying your best to share your faith. If you are not an example in this, how can you expect the congregation to enthusiastically embrace their opportunity to be an ambassador for the Lord?

"Okay, let's wrap this up until our next session in two weeks when we will get into another equally delightful subject. I'll bet you just can't wait to come together again and have me drop another heavy bomb on you, can you?"

"Well, actually, Rick," said Phil, "as scary as this is when I first hear these things, it is also a little exhilarating. I long to live a life of purpose in the Lord. I don't want our church to just continue down this path of decline and eventual death. I want things to be different! If that means we all get rather thoroughly shoved out of our comfort zone, so be it. I am sick of living a mediocre Christian life! I want my life to count for eternity!" The other board members responded,

"Whoa, way to go Phil!"

"Me too!"

"That's what I want as well!"

Rick knew that it would take some work to accomplish all this, but he was encouraged that these people wanted to make things happen. He also saw a certain satisfaction showing on the pastor's face as he realized that change was taking place in the hearts of his board members. As Rick drove home, he was again exhausted, but he was also feeling even better than he had after the last meeting with this group. They really seemed to be getting the point of what he was saying. Maybe there was some hope for Bethany Church. He longed and prayed that it would not be confined to one congregation. He desperately hoped to see an awakening of many churches all across America.

QUESTIONS FOR REFLECTION

1. Would you characterize your church as a "walking by faith" church or as a "walking by sight" church?

2. What would have to change for it to be a "walking by faith" church?

NEW VALUES FOR CHRISTIANS

RICK WAS REALLY LOOKING FORWARD TO THE NEXT MEETING WITH THE BOARD AT BETHANY CHURCH AS HE DROVE TO THEIR TOWN TWO WEEKS LATER. He was surprised at how receptive they had been to the things he had taught them. He had expected more resistance. These were, after all, some pretty radical ideas for the average church member in America. While they certainly were fearful, these folks were responding very positively. The pastor had phoned him during this last week to relate how some of the board members were taking some first tentative steps to build relationships with people who didn't know the Lord yet and were sharing their faith with them. One of Hank's friends had actually visited church that last weekend. Rick prayed for the meeting as he drove. He especially prayed that the Lord would begin to give these people at least some results from their faith and actions. He so desperately wanted to see good results happening at Bethany Church.

"Well, here we are again," Rick began. "I'm sort of surprised to see you all back after the last two sessions. I was halfway afraid we might have some people bailing out on us. But you all are showing me some courage and faith of your own to keep coming back again for more challenges.

"All right, have you all got your coffee and goodies in front of you? You're going to need them, because we have another heavy topic to deal with today," Rick said to playful groans from the folks in the room. "Here it is. Churches will not begin to grow significantly unless there is a radical restructuring of Christians' values in this country. Here's what I mean by that. God has not promised us an easy life with the big house and three-car garage and big screen HD TV. He has called us to a life as a warrior in the battle for the souls of men and women around us. This battle is strenuous. It requires sacrifice on our part. It requires risking all for the cause of Christ. If Christians in America do not get this soon and start volunteering for this army of God, we will soon face severe persecution for our faith. Then our only choices will be to renounce our Lord or join the battle. One way or another a radical restructuring of American Christians' values is coming in the near future. How much better to choose to act now before the severe persecution sets in by participating in a great awakening of God's people in this country, than to wait for persecution to refine the church? There, I've said it. What do you think of that idea?"

"Well, just exactly what do you mean?" Cindy responded. "Those seem like some pretty sweeping generalizations. Help me understand that in a little more detail."

"I'd be glad to," Rick said. "Let's break that down into a few more bite-sized chunks so we can digest it a little more easily." Someone's stomach rumbled loudly somewhere in the room as if to say, "How about lunch?" Everyone got a good laugh at that one, which gave Rick freedom to move on to his explanation.

"Here's what I mean," he continued. "We have talked about how the great majority of Christians in this country really believe that the church exists to serve them. They see their role as being a consumer of the services that the church provides, and we really can't blame them. We have spent decades training them by our actions to believe that the church exists for the Christians who are already there. We have even told them, 'We are here to serve you.' No wonder a consumer mentality has totally invaded our churches and is so pervasive in all that we do. Churches seem to be competing with each other to offer the most services so that they can attract existing Christians from other churches. We have trained Christians in this country to have a consumer-oriented mentality. That will have to change radically before the church can ever become the fighting force that the Lord intends for it to be. Here's one of the worst parts of this problem. When church attendees believe the church exists to serve them, they become totally selfish about the church. They want it to focus on them. They don't want it to focus on other people. Like spoiled children, they think that if the church puts forth great effort to reach others that means they are going to be neglected. And just like spoiled children they cry out, 'Take care of me! Don't pay any attention to those other folks! Just take care of me!' I'll tell you people, this is the biggest problem in the church today. We will never be able to make any major moves in the direction of becoming a church that is obedient to the Lord in the area of evangelism while this mentality prevails. It must be dealt with. It must be beaten down and replaced with the understanding that we are called to be servants, not to be served. The purpose of the church is to train us to be effective servants, to be able to win in the spiritual warfare we are engaged in. Somehow we have got to get Christians to wake up to this reality before it is too late.

"This mentality, probably more than any other reason, accounts for the decline of the church in America. It leads to disobedience to the Great Commission and a host of other problems, but it really starts with this mindset. What people really want the church to do is pamper them, entertain them, coddle them, and serve *them*! They don't want to hear any talk about being trained for service. They will do only what they think they have to do to maintain the Christian country club that they have joined and to which they pay their dues. It is going to take a *radical* restructuring of this value system if we have any hope of reviving a whole lot of dying churches."

"I can see how true this is both in our church and in other congregations," said Hank, "but what can we do about this? I just feel helpless when I realize how prevalent this problem has become in our church and churches throughout our nation."

"Well, let's put on our thinking caps," Rick said. "Let's do a little brainstorming. What are some ideas of what we can do to make a difference in this mindset at Bethany Church and in other churches across the nation?"

"I think we need to pray," Cindy said.

"Yes, indeed. That is probably the most important thing we can do regarding all this. We need to have individuals and groups that will engage in warfare praying for the awakening of the church. This is not just some easy five-minute session of prayer. This is the kind of praying that will be a battle for the very existence of the church in America" Rick said. "Anything else?"

"I think the pastor should preach on this subject," Phil suggested.

"What do you think about that, Pastor?" Rick asked.

"I don't see how I can avoid it," he said. "This is such an important matter that if I remain silent on it, anything else that anyone else does will have only a very minor effect on the problem. But I am going to need all the support and backing I can get when I preach on this subject. There will be people who will react rather harshly when I upset their play pens on this subject! I will probably be under attack, and there may be even some who demand that I resign from the church. Can I count on you to surround me with prayer and stand up for me when the arrows start flying?" His voice quivered a little as he asked this question. It was obvious he was genuinely concerned about the price he personally would be paying to lead this charge.

"Pastor, you can count on me. I will fight to the death with you on this one!" said Hank.

"I will be with you all the way on this one," said Cindy as she reached over and gave his shoulder a gentle rub. All the other board members expressed similar sentiments. Rick could see that they knew the price they all would pay if they sought to face this mentality head on. But the encouraging thing was that, in spite of the fact that this would be a battle in which they all would be wounded, they were signing up for duty. These people were beginning to understand just how strenuous this labor was going to be.

"What else can we do?" Rick continued.

"Well, it seems to me like we will need to take a real hard look at our programming and budgeting," Phil said. "If we are serious about this, then we need to take the action of making sure that the work of the church reflects this new direction we are hoping to set."

"Absolutely right!" Rick said. "You will need to look at every ministry department to make sure that everything you are doing as a church reflects this new reality. No more ministries that serve no greater purpose than just entertaining Christians. No more activities that are just about having fun. If the men's softball league does not get serious about infusing their program with a commitment to outreach, they will be terminated. And it isn't hard for them to include a strongly evangelistic aspect to what they are doing. They have to be held accountable to actually doing it rather than just giving lip service to it. If, at the end of the season, they show no evangelistic results the program will be discontinued. The congregation must see that we are totally serious about this emphasis throughout all that we do. If the women's Bible study program does not result in serious outreach efforts, it will be terminated. No more ministries that serve no greater purpose than just packing people's heads with Bible facts. You are going to have to make some hard decisions that people are not going to like if this is going to be the new reality for this church. Anything else that you can think of?" Rick pressed on.

"Well, I believe that all of us in this room are going to have to get real serious about living out these principles in our own lives," the pastor replied. "We can't expect people to do what we are unwilling to do ourselves. Even though this may not have been our normal practice up to this point in time, we are going to have to get serious about living as ambassadors for Christ. We are going to have to become bolder. We are going to have to stop being 'God's Secret Agents.' No more Lady Clairol Christians, only God knows for sure!" That brought some chuckles and a few loud "amens" from the rest of the folks in the room.

"You know, I am both scared and excited about doing this in my own life," Cindy said. "I am so ashamed of how I have been so ineffective as a witness for the Lord. I don't know exactly how this is all going to work out in my life, but I am determined to make this change. I am praying every morning for the Lord to lead me into contact with people who need to know him. I am praying that the Lord will give me wisdom about how to speak up for Jesus, and I am praying that the Spirit will give me the courage to be bold. I am going out of my way to spend time with my neighbors and work associates. I want to develop a loving relationship with them, and I want them to know that I know the Lord in a personal way. I am determined to be an effective ambassador for Jesus Christ!"

There were yelps of approval from the rest of the group as they also indicated they were determined to live differently in this respect. Rick almost wept as he heard these Christians awakening to the cause of Christ. Maybe there was some hope that things could be different.

"Remember," Rick cautioned the group, "we are talking about a radical restructuring of the values of the people in our churches. That will not come about easily. There will be significant battles as people resist being pushed out of their selfish, consumer-oriented mindset. Satan will throw all his forces and his most devious strategies into this battle. He will never surrender. He will persistently keep fighting back. Remember that his most common strategy is deception. He makes evil look good and good look evil. There will be some people who will genuinely believe that you are about to destroy the church with this new direction. And in a way you are. You are about to destroy the church as they have known it and replace it with something much more like the first century church.

"Remember that even a number of pastors have been sucked into the black hole of this consumer-driven church mentality. Remember I told you about the pastor who thanked his congregation for braving the rain to come to church that Sunday. Truly, the church in America has sunk to such a low point that coming to church on a Sunday when some rain is falling is the bravest thing most Christians do for the cause of Christ. We are battling to overcome a self-centered way of thinking that has completely pervaded the church. It will not be easy to root this out. It will be a battle! Unfortunately, it will at times feel like we are battling fellow Christians in this war. But that will be a deception. We are really battling the evil one who has deceived the vast majority of Christ followers in this country. We must continually keep that in mind. Don't ever allow yourself to start thinking that the people are the enemy. They are the victims of the enemy and his schemes to deceive.

"Remember what Jesus taught. The way to joy is to lose ourselves in obedience to the Lord. If we try to protect our life, we end up losing it, but if we lose our life for Christ's sake, we gain it. By allowing this consumer mentality to prevail in our churches we are consigning thousands, even millions of Christians to a life of misery. We are denying them the joy of a life lived in full surrender and service to the Lord. In a very real way we are fighting for the lives of the very people who will resist our efforts to change this culture. We can set them free from the self-inflicted unhappiness that always results when Christians choose the way of trying to save their lives. When we try to find happiness in our own strength and through our own resources we always get emptiness and misery. When we desperately cling to our lives in an attempt to wring all the pleasure out of them we can we end up frustrated. But that is the way of our culture. In so many ways we are told again and again that 'You only go around once. You've got to grab for all the gusto you can get!' Unfortunately, way too many Christians have bought into that philosophy without even realizing that they have done so. The problem is, the more miserable they become pursuing a course the Lord promised would make them miserable, the more they blame the church for their misery and demand that the church give them more of what made them miserable in the first place. By doing what we are doing we have the hope of setting these people free from the vicious cycle of pursuing pleasure and getting misery. This approach to Christian living always results in squabbles and divisions in the church. Each Christian is demanding that their desires be met by the church. Often those desires are in direct conflict with the desires of another Christian, so squabbling and turf protecting become the order of the day in a church where the consumer driven mentality prevails. If and when those Christians become fellow soldiers in the cause of Christ, they will be fighting shoulder to shoulder against the enemy, not against each other like so many children trying to get the most candy they can from the broken *piñata*. We can help Christians enter a life characterized by fullness of joy!

"Folks, I am so proud of you!" Rick affirmed the people. "You have clearly come to understand what is at stake in this battle. You are counting the cost you will have to pay in waging this war, and you are still signing up for duty. I will be praying for you and supporting you. I am as near as a phone call or an e-mail. Contact me any time you need to talk. We are fellow soldiers in this war and we must, absolutely must, support one another. Never let any bit of ego slip into this. This is not about us, how righteous we are, how much more spiritual we are than any other Christian, or how much more understanding we have. I don't know exactly why the Lord has chosen you and me for this battle. It isn't because we are better than others. But he has chosen us, so let's be the best warriors we can be through his strength that empowers us. Okay, let's break for lunch, and I will start a new subject when we get back."

QUESTIONS FOR REFLECTION

1. Are there any ways that your values, personally, would need to change for you to be in line with God's plan for the church?

2. What would it cost you to make those changes?

FOLLOW THE LEADER

AFTER LUNCH, RICK STARTED AGAIN WITH MORE HEAVY WORDS, "SECOND TO THE ALL-PERVASIVE CONSUMER MENTALITY, THERE HAS PROBABLY BEEN NOTHING THAT HAS HINDERED THE CHURCH IN ITS CAUSE MORE THAN AN UNWILLINGNESS TO FOLLOW LEADERS. In some ways it is very much related to the consumer mentality and flows out of it. When we are all demanding our own way, when we think the church should be all about us, we are unwilling to trust anyone to lead us who has not made a total pledge to see to our individual happiness. That is such a major problem in our country at this time. Way too many people are demanding that the government take care of them without ever giving any thought to who is going to pay for it. Way too many people are assuming that 'the rich people' should be responsible for taking care of them. Anyone seeking elected office had better promise these people that their 'needs' will be taken care of at someone else's expense in order to have any hope of being elected. We have a similar problem going on in the church. Unless a leader very obviously commits himself to taking care of every 'need' that the people express, he won't be followed. Of course, we all know that what people call 'needs' are in most cases just their desires to be pampered and entertained. True leaders who challenge the people to live as servants for the Lord are regarded as 'uncaring' about the needs of the congregation.

"But, this is not what the Bible teaches about how the church is to do its business," Rick emphasized. "Over and over again in the Bible we see examples of the fact that when God wants something done he always starts by raising up one individual. God never raised up a committee. He called one person, implanted the vision in that person, who then passed that vision to others who caught the vision and joined the cause. That one person didn't operate as a law unto himself, but he was clearly the leader that God had appointed. This is also the case in all the great things the Lord is doing in our day as well. Every dynamically growing church has a pastor who is clearly the leader of the church. Every para-church movement has begun when God placed the vision in the heart of one person who then spread the vision to others who joined in the cause. Just look at examples such as Bill Bright, Billy Graham, Rick Warren, James Dobson, and Bill Hybels. In every case that I am aware of in which God has worked powerfully in our own day, he has called one person to be the leader who then inspired others to join in the cause. I'm not talking about a pastor being a dictator who ignores all insight from his elders, but in our local churches this idea is resisted tooth and nail. There is near total misunderstanding over this question of who is to lead.

"There are two profoundly important questions that every church and every Christian must answer. The right answers will result in a healthy, growing congregation. The wrong answers result in a stunted church and miserable Christians. The two questions are, 1) Why does the church exist? And, 2) Who is in charge here? We have spent a lot of time on the first question. The typical answer that is given to the question 'Why does the church exist?' is 'to serve me, to make me happy, to devote itself to satisfying my every need.' The biblical answer to this question is that the church exists to serve God and do his will, the most important part of which is to reach lost people with the gospel and to lead all Christians to become obedient and faithful disciples of Jesus Christ. With regard to the second question several answers are typically given. In some churches the answer to 'Who's in charge here?' is 'We are all in charge. This is a democracy.' That is especially true of denominations like this one which historically have been strongly congregational in our form of government. In some other churches there is a tendency to say,

'The elders are in charge.' But in almost no churches will the people answer that the pastor is in charge. The pastor needs to walk in mutual submission with the elders, meaning that he doesn't take action until they agree, and they don't take action until he agrees. But it needs to be clearly understood by all that he is the leader of the congregation.

"In most churches," Rick continued, "the members of the churches and their duly elected officials resist pastoral leadership because they want to be in charge. They want to control the church and the decisions that it makes. Why is this so important to these people? It starts to look suspiciously like it comes from a desire to make sure the church does what they want it to do. They want to control the outcome so their 'needs' will be met. But the pastor, in most cases, has a different agenda. His first priority is not taking care of the 'needs' of the people. He knows that most of what they call needs are really just their desires to be entertained, pampered, coddled, and made to feel important. There are so many people in our churches who use their position of service or leadership to gain self-esteem. Those people will do anything to protect their turf, to make sure they are able to continue being a big fish in a small pond. Of course that attitude makes it particularly difficult for the pastor to lead. He can't change anything, even if the church desperately needs the change, because any change will threaten someone's little personal kingdom."

"But don't we have to be concerned that a pastor will abuse that kind of authority?" Phil asked. Rick was sure that Phil sincerely believed it to be a serious concern.

"Okay, but think of this," Rick responded, "in virtually every church someone occupies this position of primary leader. If it isn't the pastor, then that position is filled by a layman who acts as the 'church boss.' I can think of no exceptions to this rule in my experience. Either the pastor is the primary leader of the church or a 'church boss' is the primary leader. Now tell me, why would you trust a 'church boss' to fill that role so much more than trusting the pastor in that role? The 'church boss' has no training, no experience, no expertise, and very little to lose if the church fails. The pastor usually has had extensive training, years of experience, a great deal of expertise, and everything to lose if the church fails. In addition to that, he has already paid a heavy price just to be in the ministry. In my case, I left behind the opportunity to be in medical school, with all the prestige and financial rewards that occupation promises, in order to become a pastor. The 'church boss' has paid no price. In my experience, I have never seen a 'church boss' who had the best interests of the church as their primary motivation. I have never once seen a church boss lead a church in the direction of greater effectiveness in outreach. Never, in my experience, has their influence in the church resulted in more people coming to faith in Jesus and growing stronger in the Lord. Their influence has never been about obedience to the Lord in the most basic commands he has given us. It has always been about their ego, power, influence, and turf. And yet, over and over again, I have seen churches choose to follow the 'church boss' rather than follow the pastor. 'Church bosses' are usually effective manipulators. Very few pastors engage in that kind of thing. Most of them hate the politics that so frequently shows up in the work of the church. They, with few exceptions, are genuinely motivated to care for the people as well as further the cause of Christ. Are there some who do not live up to this high calling? Of course! Anytime human beings are involved there is that potential. But, I have to say, I know of no cases where the 'church boss' had the high calling and motivation of the pastor. Sometimes the 'church boss' has around him a group of people. Sometimes they are even the elders or board of the church. In those cases you have the dictatorship of a few, instead of one church boss. Why is that preferable to the man whom God has called to lead the congregation, leading the church?"

"Yes, but what happens if a pastor does go off the rails or gets into things he shouldn't?" Cindy asked.

"Okay, what happens if a church boss is leading the church in a direction contrary to the will of God? I contend that it is a whole lot easier to get rid of a pastor who loses his way, than a church boss who never found the way. Most churches have clearly outlined procedures to get rid of a pastor. In addition to all the formal means to get rid of a pastor, there are a hundred devious methods to force the pastor to resign. And don't forget something—ultimately God holds the pastor accountable. He can and will end the ministry of an errant pastor. His means of doing so are completely unlimited. He will not tolerate a pastor who abuses his position.

"But the church seems all too willing to tolerate a church boss who stifles the work of the church. Usually the church boss doesn't call the people to accountability and urge them to obedience to the Lord like the pastor does. His leadership is preferable to that of a pastor who tries to galvanize the people into action obeying the Lord. Usually he, or sometimes she, is content to lead the people to join his little army within the church to oppose the leadership of the pastor. Folks, it's time to wake up! We have such a big concern about a pastor who might abuse his position, but we routinely tolerate church bosses who prevent the work of the Lord from flourishing!

"Are you aware that eighteen to twenty thousand pastors are leaving the ministry each year due to burnout, frustration, and abusive treatment by their congregations? And of those that remain in the ministry, fifty percent would like to leave but are afraid they can't make a living elsewhere.[4] Wake up, folks! We are witnessing a slaughter of the prophets in our day that makes the Old Testament slaughter of the prophets by God's people, the Israelites, seem small in comparison. This has been the pattern of God's people throughout the Bible. Over and over again, God's people have rebelled against the leader God has sent. You might say, 'That was just in the Old Testament.' If that is true, why did the Lord, speaking through the Apostle Paul, feel it necessary to give us the instructions of Hebrews 13:17-18, 'Obey your leaders and submit to their authority. They keep watch over you as men who must give an account. Obey them so that their work will be a joy, not a burden, for that would be of no advantage to you'? Apparently in New Testament times as well, there was a tendency to rebel against the leader God had chosen to lead a given church.

"Notice the strong language used in this passage. God says *obey* your leaders and *submit* to their *authority*. They must give account to the Lord. Again, he used the word *obey* a second time. How can we possibly avoid the point the Lord is making? Pastors are not to be people who just make suggestions. They are to lead with authority, and the people are to obey that authority. I do not recommend that a pastor act unilaterally. He should rely on his board or elders for input and take it seriously. But it is clear in the Scriptures that God expects the people of the church to have a heart set on following the pastor's leadership.

"Look around you," Rick said. "Every team has a leader. The teams that have a good leader win, and the teams with a poor leader lose. That is as true in business as it is in sports. It applies to every human organization. Why in the world has the church developed this idea that it can function as a leaderless organization? It is complete nonsense. That doesn't work in any part of human society, and it doesn't work in the church. It is time we start recognizing that God has commanded us to follow our leaders.

"God's method has always been to raise up a person into whom he poured the vision of what he wanted accomplished. That person then went to the people of God to inspire them to do what God was directing them all to do. Far too often, the people God wanted to inspire to action, through the person he had chosen to lead, turned against the person God had sent. Sometimes they killed that person; sometimes they imprisoned him or her; sometimes they just ignored that person. The pattern we are seeing in our churches has been going on since God first chose to himself a people he called 'Israel.' Just look how often the people blamed Moses for the things God was leading the people to experience. They wanted to stone Moses on several occasions. Folks, if we understand our biblical history, we shouldn't be so concerned that the leader will stray! We should be far more concerned about the people who oppose the leader and, in so doing, oppose God! That has been a far more common occurrence throughout biblical and current history! That is how Satan has usually worked in the history of God's people. Wake up, people! If we are unwilling to follow the person God has chosen to lead us, how do you think the Lord is going to get his work done? This is the method he has always followed both in Bible times and today. This unwillingness to follow the leadership of the pastor is one of the biggest reasons for the terrible condition of the church today!"

"Wow, I never thought of it that way," Cindy responded. "But I can see that you are right. No wonder you get so worked up about this. You see the carnage in pastors' lives because of this way of thinking. And you see the damage it causes in our churches. We have got to somehow get our people to start thinking differently on this matter."

"Let me put it this way," Rick said. "For the church to come awake again, we are once again going to have to start living by the biblical pattern of following the leader that God chooses to lead his people.

"Very closely related to this, we need to pray that God will raise up leaders for the church, not just caretakers. Due to a number of influences, we have seen several generations of pastors who have had a very weak understanding of their role in the church. There have been so many voices saying pastors should be caretakers and teachers, but not leaders. That has resulted in pastors who are keepers of the aquarium, not fishers of men; pastors who value peace and harmony in the church above obedience to the Great Commission. It has resulted in pastors who are not agonizing over the failure of the church to reach thousands, even millions of people with the gospel. Our churches are dying for lack of leaders willing to storm the gates of hell to deliver lost people from the clutches of Satan. This has become a very vicious cycle. Church people, in most cases, are unwilling to follow strong leaders, and they run them out of their churches. Instead they replace them with men who are just teachers and caretakers. So that is the model of being a pastor that most young people have seen. Not surprisingly, the young men who are attracted to the ministry by seeing that model of pastoral ministry are those who by temperament are teachers and caretakers. Young men who are entrepreneurial leaders see the common model of being a pastor and say, 'That's just not me.' And it isn't them. Those who are strong leaders are being discouraged from entering the ministry just because of the models of pastors that they see. There are some rare exceptions to this generalization, but just not enough to have an impact on the church as a whole. Unfortunately, some of those with entrepreneurial gifts are enticed to use those gifts in the competition to attract Christians from other churches by offering more and better services. We have got to be praying for the Lord to raise up people for the ministry who are passionate about the cause of Christ, not just the country club for Christians.

"There is another close corollary to this," Rick continued. "The laypeople in our churches must begin to see themselves as laborers in the fields that are white unto harvest. They have got to stop seeing themselves first as nursery workers or small group leaders. And they especially must stop seeing themselves as consumers of the services of the church. They must start seeing themselves as warriors in the battle between Christ and Satan. They must begin to see themselves as the people, the only people in the world, who have the key that will open the gates of hell and set billions of people free. There are millions of Christians in America. If they will just start seeing themselves as warriors, not consumers, the church can again be powerful in spreading the gospel. Jesus told us in Matthew 9:37-38, 'Then he said to his disciples, "The harvest is plentiful but the workers are few. Ask the Lord of the harvest, therefore, to send out workers into his harvest field."' How important do you think it is in our day that we be fervently praying for God to raise up millions of Christians in America who see their role as harvesters, as warriors, not just consumers?" Rick beseeched them. "It will take millions of Christians who recognize what their primary task in this life is. We need millions who will recognize that they are only in this life for a short time, and only during that short time will they have the privilege of bringing people to faith in Jesus. We need millions who will recognize that the main reason they were left on earth after they accepted Christ is to lead others to faith in Jesus. Please be praying earnestly every day that God would raise up millions of people who will be laborers in the harvest fields.

"Okay, I have given you enough to think about for one day," Rick concluded. "I look forward to seeing you all again in two weeks. During this next two weeks I strongly encourage you to begin praying that the Lord would raise up laborers for the harvest fields. And I encourage you to begin praying that pastors would be raised up who are leaders in the cause of Christ, not just servants in the country club of Christ."

Rick was pleased that these folks on the board at Bethany Church seemed to be responding as positively as they were. This was heavy material he was laying on them. It was nothing short of destroying church as they had known it all their lives and replacing it with something none of them had ever seen or experienced. Amazingly, they were still with him and really seemed to be understanding what he was saying. More importantly, they seemed to believe he was speaking the truth.

QUESTIONS FOR REFLECTION

1. Does your church in any way limit your pastor from being the leader the church needs?

2. What will need to change in your church for the pastor to have real freedom to lead the church?

WEEK FIVE
STUDY GUIDE

1. Have group members share any experiences they have had in sharing the gospel with others. Especially have them explain the emotions they felt before, during, and after this experience. Is there anyone in your church who is actively being a witness on a regular basis?

2. Have individual members take ten minutes or less to answer the question: What will have to change in my life for me to be an effective witness for Jesus? Report back to the group.

3. Have the group break into subgroups of three or four and brainstorm possible first, second, and third date activities appropriate for your congregation. Come back and share your ideas with the whole group.

4. Discuss together whether your church is a "walking by faith" church or a "walking by sight" church. What would have to change for it to become a "walking by faith" church?

5. Take five minutes for the individuals in the group to answer the question: Is there any way that my values, personally, would need to change for me to be in line with God's plan for the church? Then gather and have each person share their answer with the whole group.

6. Bring a copy of the church's calendar for the month for each person. Break into groups of three or four. Have one group divide up the activities of the church on the calendar according to whether they are focused on maintenance or growth. Have another group divide by whether the activities focus on "committee work" or "the Lord's work." Have another group divide the activities by whether they focus outward or inward. Have each group assign percentages to each type of activities. Discuss as a whole group which activities should be dropped and which should be continued in order to accomplish the real purpose of the church.

7. Discuss as a whole group if there are any ways the church limits the pastor from being the leader the church needs. Are there people who are hindering him from doing so? Is there anyone functioning as a "church boss"?

WEEK SIX

CULTURAL RELEVANCY

"**ALL RIGHT, HERE WE ARE ONCE AGAIN,**" **RICK BEGAN THIS SESSION WITH THE BOARD AT BETHANY CHURCH.** "I hope I can get this all wrapped up today. This has been a long haul, and you have been nothing short of amazing. I am so grateful for your attention and the fact that you seem to be understanding what I am saying. Even more importantly, you seem to believe what I am saying and seem willing to do something about it."

"What you are saying makes sense," Phil said. "It explains so many things that I haven't understood. It has frustrated me that so many churches are declining but I have not known why that is so or what to do about it. It is very sobering to realize that all of us have been part of the problem, not part of the solution. My prayer is that before my life ends I can be part of turning this thing around. I pray that in my lifetime I will have the privilege of seeing churches come awake, instead of seeing churches dying."

"I pray that all of us will have that privilege," Rick responded enthusiastically. "Now let's deal with several last but no less important principles today. For the church to begin to reach millions of people for Christ, we are going to have to make sure we are culturally relevant. The church has slipped so far away from this principle that the world looks at us almost like we are some weird cult. America has changed so rapidly that it is a foreign culture to anyone who tries to live in the way the Lord has instructed us to live. If we are going to be warriors in the battle for the souls of millions of lost people around us, that means we are going to have to communicate the message in a way that is relevant to the culture around us. It means we are going to have to see ourselves as missionaries. Missionaries in other countries realize that they have to relate to the people they hope to reach in keeping with the culture in which they live. They cannot expect that the people will first adapt to the American culture in order that the gospel can be presented to them with all its American cultural trappings. The missionary adapts to the culture of the people. He doesn't change the truth of the gospel, and he doesn't adopt the moral values of the culture that conflict with biblical standards. But in all the ways that are morally neutral, the missionary adapts to the culture of the people he hopes to reach. We American Christians are going to have to do the very same thing in order to reach this culture that has become increasingly foreign to the culture of the church. It has been said 'If the rate of change outside an organization exceeds the rate of change inside the organization, the organization is dying.'

"The degree to which we have been unwilling to adapt to the culture is a reflection of the consumer mentality so prevalent in our churches. If we see the church as existing to meet our desires then, of course, we want to stay comfortable. We don't want to have to upset our safe, comfortable, little world for anyone. We really don't care about those people outside of the church. If they want to go to hell that is their choice, just let us enjoy our little club for Christians. That has been the mentality of most Christians in most churches. We may give lip service to the idea of outreach, but that is all it is. The minute someone tries to change the church in ways that will make it more effective in outreach, we squawk as though they are trying to kill the church. But we must make these changes or our churches will actually die."

"Okay, what are some of those changes we have to make?" Hank asked.

"I was just about to go there," Rick responded. "The first change relates to style issues. We want to make sure that we don't appear weird to the world around us in ways that are purely matters of style, things about which the Bible doesn't require us to be one way or the other, for example, things such as style of music. In spite of the fact that bloody battles have been fought over this issue, the Bible gives us no instruction as to one style of music being holier than any other. What we do know is that during times when the church was very effective in reaching lost people, they chose to sing and play music that sounded very much like the secular music of their time. Often they took the musical score from secular songs and added Christian words. Even when they wrote the notes as well as the words, they chose to write notes that sounded like the secular music of the day. If the musical sound is strange to people's ears, they won't hear the words. But if the sound is familiar to what they have been listening to every day, it is easy for them to listen to and hear the Christian words. It is amazing to me how quickly we find a type of music that we really like and then label it as the only 'godly' music. Even with the contemporary Christian music that is being used in so many churches now we must continually keep asking the question, 'Does this sound similar to the musical sound people are hearing every day?' If we don't, we will just develop another type of music that we cling to after the world has moved on to something else. Being culturally relevant requires of us continual change. Remember, the culture around us changes with every generation. The church must be prepared, even eager, to change in style issues to fit the culture around us. Some churches are still fighting the battle about adapting to the Baby Boomer Generation's style. They are way behind the curve. Now churches must be adapting to the culture of the Digital Generation. This generation is dominated by a lack of trust in large institutions that are too 'slick', and characterized by the prevailing mentality that there are no absolutes. The church will have to adapt to that culture in order to reach it. But that is what the Lord has instructed us to do anyway. When the Bible instructs us to 'be transformed,' to continually mature in the Lord, it is telling us to continually change. The Lord has no intention that we reach a level of Christian maturity and then not change any more. He intends for us to be continually maturing. That requires continual change. To resist change is to resist what God has promised he will do in our lives."

"But I don't like that new music!" gruffed one of the older members of the board. "That stuff has no theology to it! It all sounds the same to me! Are you telling me we are going to have to put up with that junk? I don't like that stuff, and I'm not going to listen to it! I will leave this church and go somewhere that has good old Christian music like I have known and loved for sixty-five years if you make us have to listen to that trash!"

"As I was listening to you, all I heard you say was 'I, I, I,'" Rick said. "Remember, for the church to be effective in reaching unchurched people, we have to adapt to the culture around us in style issues. That is going to require some of us to adjust to a new kind of music. I know it won't be easy, but we are going to have to do this or our churches are just going to die."

"I don't care what you say!" the older member was almost yelling now. "I'm not going to have my church doing rock music in the worship service! That is sacrilegious! And I am really mad at you for telling me I should put up with this nonsense! We have to preserve our heritage! My wife has sung in the choir here for fifty-nine years! I'm not going to have you kicking dirt on all those years of faithful service she has put in! And don't think I am alone in this! There are plenty of others who just will not put up with this nonsense!" At this point the objector left the room in a great huff.

"Well, folks," Rick followed the trauma with words of reality, "we didn't really expect that everyone would be all excited about this did we? We have to expect that some folks will have a really hard time making this adjustment. But let's continue to pray for him daily and reach out to him in love to see if he can be brought to an understanding of why this is so important. Okay?

"Style issues also relate to things like the way we dress and the language we use. As long as we are not disobeying the Lord in issues like modesty, we should try to dress like the world around us. There is no virtue in looking different from the people around us in any way the Lord has not commanded. Our language is especially important in being relevant. It is so easy to speak a type of 'Christianese' that the world around finds confusing or silly. In order to reach lost people we need to be spending time with them anyway. When we do that, let's pay attention to the language they are using. If it is not ungodly let's adopt the language of the people around us. It does not harm the cause of Christ if we use a slang expression common in our day. It actually helps the cause of Christ as long as this isn't some form of crude or God-dishonoring speech.

"The place this probably shows up most strongly is in our preaching. The Bible touches on every area of life. There is no part of life that the Bible doesn't address either by direct promises or commands or by general principles. When we preach, we want to make sure that every week we are dealing with the real issues of life, not just some bit of theology or biblical truth with no attempt made to relate it to the real world experiences of people, believer and unbeliever alike. Once when I finished preaching, a man who had not yet accepted Christ walked up to me and said, 'Have you been talking to my wife?' Because the Word of God was being preached with strong application to everyday life, it began to speak very personally to him, so much so that it felt like someone had been telling me about his own personal issues. Within a few weeks he had come to faith in Christ. Often other people in the church expressed a similar sentiment.

"When we work hard to apply the truth of God's Word to the everyday experiences of people around us, be they believers or not yet believers, God speaks into their lives. When our preaching is culturally relevant, the person who attends church but has not yet believed in Jesus feels God speaking to him or her. They soon understand that the Lord cares about every part of their life. It is far more likely they will accept Christ than if they came to church and the pastor droned on about some unapplied bit of theology. All theology has its application to life. It is the job of the preacher to make sure that he makes that application loud and clear. It is laziness to just state biblical or theological truth and expect the people to make the application themselves. It is the job of the preacher, before he ever presents a message, to make sure that he fully understands the interface between this biblical principle and the culture around him. Then it is his job to make sure that he has made this application very clear. Whether he is preaching expositorily or topically, he still has the same assignment. He must make sure he has strongly applied God's truth to real life experiences. I always used to ask myself a question before I ever preached a message," said Rick. "That question is 'So what?' So what difference does this make in real life? If I couldn't answer that question, I knew that the message was not yet ready to preach. If I did not yet see how this message touched on some important area of daily life, I had more work to do before I presented it. Before I ever preached a message I knew what

I expected the people to do in response to this message. If I focused on people remembering what I said, I got discouraged. They actually remembered very few of the details I preached. I did not preach for retention. I preached for transformation. Over time I saw many lives transformed in significant ways. That is the great joy of being a preacher.

"If people can listen to our preaching and not feel challenged to make some changes in their lives, we are not going to be very effective in reaching anyone, especially lost people. The Lord, if we read his Word consistently, is frequently challenging us to make changes in our lives. Our preaching needs to reflect that emphasis. When we show people that the Lord promises to produce good results in their lives, if they make the changes he is calling them to make, they are very likely to make those changes. The first of those changes is to put their faith in Jesus alone for the forgiveness of their sins. Preaching that is relevant to the life experiences of believers and unbelievers alike makes the church very effective in reaching lost people.

"Even the way we build and decorate our church buildings should reflect our desires to relate to the un-churched person," Rick continued. "The Old Testament tabernacle and temple were not constructed with any thought to reaching out to people outside the people of God. They were designed and built for the believers only. So we make a mistake in assuming that our church buildings should have that same sacred feel today. In the Old Testament, God met the priests in a special way in the tabernacle or temple. In the New Testament, the Holy Spirit lives in every believer. We no longer have a sacred building where God meets us in a special way. The high school gymnasium or the movie theater can be every bit as much of a place for God to work as a church building. Some of the most effective churches in America do not meet in typical church buildings. They meet in a much more 'secular' looking type of facility. We hinder the spread of the gospel when we make our buildings in such a way that they feel weird to un-churched people. We advance the spread of the gospel when our buildings are very welcoming and feel very comfortable to someone who does not attend church on any regular basis. This can be one more way for the church to be culturally relevant. I think if our church buildings look too 'churchy,' it hinders the spreading of the gospel. We should be more focused on designing church buildings that are much more efficient, with multi-purpose spaces. Let's design them so that the worship space is also a gymnasium and a fellowship hall. Why spend all that money on a space that only gets used two or three hours a week when we can design a space that is every bit as effective for worship, but can be used every day of the week for other purposes as well? And when the un-churched person attends a Sunday or Friday or Saturday service there it won't feel so strange to him or her. It will feel much more welcoming and comfortable to them.

"What I am saying"—Rick drove home this point—"is that we have to take a long hard look at everything we do as a church. We need to ask ourselves, 'How is this going to look or feel to the un-churched person?' We should try to take the most objective look possible at our worship services. Are there a lot of inside jokes, so to speak, that will make the visitor feel like an outsider? Are there practices that just feel strange to someone who is not part of the 'in crowd'? I think the way we receive the offering and participate in the Lord's supper are two areas that have high potential for seeming weird to unbelievers. While Christians may grow accustomed to every person coming forward to put their offering in the plate, it puts the visitor in a particularly awkward spot. The same goes for receiving communion. Long periods of silence while people meditate make the visitor uncomfortable. Anytime a response is expected of the congregation, that the visitor is unaware of, it makes him or her feel like a real outsider. These things put the visitor in the position of wondering uneasily, 'What's going to happen next?' They can't really settle in and feel comfortable since they are on edge wondering what will be expected of them next. We really don't want our guests to have that uneasy feeling. We want them to feel welcomed and very comfortable without putting any spotlight on them. They want to feel that they can blend in without standing out as 'the new person' who doesn't know what he or she is doing. So many churches obviously give no thought to how their building or their service will feel to the person who is coming in from the outside. Some even seem to pride themselves on having something very unique, without giving any thought to how the first-timer will feel in the midst of this 'uniqueness.'

"Cultural relevancy is all about really understanding what the actual needs and interests of the un-churched person are. It will show up in our programming. If we care about reaching people with the gospel, we will have programs designed with their needs or interests in mind. We will have programs to meet their real needs for help in parenting, marriage, divorce recovery, personal financial management, job searching, time management, and a host of other programs that deal with real needs of real people. The people already in our churches have all those same needs and will be greatly blessed also by this type of program. Cultural relevancy is not some difficult thing. It just takes some careful thought. Most of all it requires us to realize the church is not all about 'me.' It requires me to realize the church is, first and foremost, about others. If we honestly put ourselves into the shoes of the un-churched person and try to design all that we do with their interests in mind we will greatly enhance the effectiveness of our outreach. For those of us who are older, we will need to make a point of meeting with and really understanding the mindset of the Digital Generation." Rick paused and took a deep breath. He looked around the room at all the thoughtful faces and then said, "All right, who is ready for some lunch?" Rick asked. "Some pizza has been provided and salad and drinks. Help yourself. We have one more important subject to deal with when we come back."

They all wandered off down the hall to a room where food had been set up.

Later, Rick was pleased to see how earnestly they all were discussing the things they had been learning over these last weeks of his teaching. It was clear that they were taking this very seriously.

QUESTIONS FOR REFLECTION

1. In what ways might our church seem "weird" to an un-churched person?

2. How attached am I to those things?

REPENTANCE

AFTER EVERYONE HAD ENJOYED THE PIZZA, RICK CONVENED THEM AGAIN. "Let's get going on this last and maybe most important thing I have to share," said Rick. "All of the things we have talked about are critically important. But there is one thing I have come to believe is even more important than all the rest. Unless there is genuine repentance on the part of God's people in America, the church will continue to die. We Christians in this country have sinned grievously against the Lord, and until we recognize that, within ourselves and to the Lord, we will remain powerless. All the new methods or techniques will have only limited effectiveness until we recognize our selfish disobedience to the command of the Lord. He has commanded us to make disciples of as many people as we possibly can in the shortest time we possibly can.

"We have chosen instead to make the church our private club. We have demanded that the church be all about us. We have developed a model of church that keeps us entertained, pampered, coddled, and keeps our own egos stroked. We have participated in probably the greatest slaughter of the prophets in human history by running off any pastors who teach in a way that threatens our cozy little church club. We have given no thought to the destruction we have wreaked in their lives and the lives of their families. Way too many pastor's kids have grown up with the knowledge that the church can be the cruelest bunch of people on earth. Like spoiled children, we have demanded our own way and thrown temper tantrums if anyone threatened to take our toys away from us for our own good. Probably most damning of all is that we have regarded the way we have done church as the way it should be done. We have been very self-righteous about it all. We have honestly believed that we were doing a service to God by insisting on this kind of church. We have been self-righteously sure of our way of doing things to the point of regarding pastors who have tried to awaken the church as heretics or wild-eyed radicals. In reality, they were just being more like the first century church was.

"Our sin against the Lord has been so grievous that I do not believe he will again empower the church with his great power unless we repent. I do not believe that he will cause great things to occur in the church until his people fall on their faces in recognition of their great sin. Never were the words of 2 Chronicles 7:14 more true, 'If my people, who are called by my name, will humble themselves and pray and seek my face and turn from their wicked ways, then will I hear from heaven and will forgive their sin and will heal their land.' This cannot be an academic exercise. This must come from the heart and result in a great brokenness among Christians throughout this land." Rick was really getting wound up on this when he noticed Cindy sniffling and crying softly.

"Cindy, what's wrong?" he asked.

"We have been so selfish and sinful!" she blurted out. "How could we get so far away from what the Lord has called us to be and do? My heart is breaking as I think of the ways I have disobeyed the Lord and broken his heart! I am so sorry for my part in creating a church that has failed the Lord in just about every way!"

Rick barely had time to hear what she was saying before Hank, the blustering tough guy, was on his knees by his chair bawling loudly as he sobbed out his confession before the Lord, "Oh, Lord, I have failed you so miserably! I got so wrapped up in myself that I completely forgot what your great purpose is in this world! I have ignored lost people all around me, people who are going to an eternity in the presence of Satan! Oh, Lord, forgive me! I know you have forgiven me, but please use my life and make a difference through me now. I surrender all my selfish desires to you. I just want to be used of you in a powerful way! Before it's too late, please, move throughout this church and wake all of us up."

Soon everyone in the room was kneeling by their chairs crying out to God. Everyone was confessing their failures and asking the Lord to work in power in their lives. Some were sobbing loudly. Others were sniffling softly. But all were utterly sincere as they confessed their failures to the Lord and cried out for him to use them in a powerful way. The pastor was crying also, but there was a joyful smile through his tears as he thanked the Lord for this day and asked the Lord to guide him as he guided this bunch of people to a new day in the church.

Rick was completely taken off guard by this. He had not been expecting this reaction, but as he thought about it he realized that the Lord was beginning to answer the prayers he and the other two superintendents had been raising for months and even years. Exhilaration grew inside him as he recognized what was happening.

"Oh, Lord," he prayed, "thank you for what you are doing here. Please let this be the beginning of something great. Please act, Lord, to awaken Christians throughout this land. Please give me wisdom as to what I should do next. This is completely new territory for me, but I know you have promised to guide me. I just thank you for bringing this day to pass."

After about fifteen minutes of this, the room began to quiet down, and people came off their knees and sat in their chairs. A number began to hug each other and Rick.

"That was amazing!" Hank said. "I felt the presence of the Lord like never before."

"I am so filled with joy," Cindy commented. "I am so sorry for my sinful attitude about the church, but I feel the forgiveness of the Lord so profoundly today. I never want to go back to living in that sinful way again. I don't ever want to be so selfish again. I want to make a difference in this church. I can't just stand by and watch it die anymore." Loud "amens" rang out from the others. Rick could see that they really meant it.

"One last thing I want to encourage you about," Rick said. "We don't want this to be confined to just the eight of us in this room. We want this to spread throughout this church and throughout our nation. It will take a nation-wide awakening of the church if there is any hope of getting out of the mess the church is in throughout our land. Pray that the kind of brokenness you experienced today will be experienced by pastors and laypeople throughout our country. If God answers our prayers, great things can come about. The church can be revived. And when that happens, our nation will experience a profound transformation. Millions of people will come to faith in the Lord who never knew him. When that happens, it will have a powerful effect on our nation. No amount of legislation can bring our nation back from the brink as long as the vast majority of the people are determined to live godless lives. But if more and more people trust in Jesus and begin to bring their lives into conformity with the Lord's plan for them, it will have a wonderful effect on our nation. This kind of thing has happened before here in America and in the United Kingdom. Please pray that it will happen again.

"I believe that methods and systems are important and can bring about some good results. We should by all means use the best methods, systems, and principles available to us. But that isn't enough. Unless God acts like he did here today on a much broader scale, the best methods and systems will fail. Unless God brings pastors, other church leaders, and the laypeople to the point of falling on our faces before almighty God in sorrowful repentance, the church in America will continue on its sinful path until severe persecution is required to purify the church. We must be beseeching the Lord to act this way in many more churches.

"Well, there isn't much more I need to say today. I am rejoicing with you that the Lord has done something powerful here today, but it is only a beginning. Devote yourselves to prayer daily for this church and the churches throughout our nation. Ask the Lord to clearly show you what he wants you to do next. Pastor, would it be okay if we meet again in two weeks just to check in and see what the Lord is doing with each one of us?"

"I would like that very much," the pastor said. "And can I be in touch with you between now and then as anything arises?"

"That would be great," said Rick. "This is all new territory for me, too. I have been praying for this for a long time, and today represents a small beginning. It is small, but it definitely is a beginning. I thank you all for the privilege of being with you when the Lord worked in this way."

"Thank you for your work with us," said Phil. "You have been the catalyst the Lord has used to start something wonderful here. I pray that this is only the beginning of something greater than just the eight of us in this room."

Rick hugged each one as he left that day and whispered words of God's grace in their ears. He drove home in a state of amazement. Had God really begun to answer the prayers he had been raising up for so long? It certainly appeared that he had. Rick began sobbing out words of thanks to the Lord as he realized the magnitude of what had happened that day. He could barely see to drive—the tears of joy were coming so fast.

When he walked into the house, Marilyn could tell something had happened. She could see the look of pure joy on his face. He grabbed her, swung her around, and danced her around the kitchen. So what if she had recovered from back surgery only six months ago. This was a day for celebration!

"What is it?" she said. It took a good hour for Rick to relate to her all he had taught them over the last months and especially what had happened today. She was having a hard time taking it all in since she hadn't been there. But the more she heard the more her heart rose up in celebration. She had lived with Rick's obsession for the awakening of the church for so long that it had become hers also. Now she was able to experience the joy along with him. They knelt right there by the kitchen table in joyful prayers of thanksgiving.

The next delightful part of Rick's agenda was to phone his buddies who had been praying for this day with him. He got them on a conference call later that evening. Al was in a hotel near one of the churches he would speak at tomorrow. Wayne was home recovering from the flu, but he was well enough to get in on this call. Rick had to relate the whole story again, but he never tired of telling it. It just gave him one more opportunity to rejoice in the goodness of the Lord's actions that day. The guys had plenty of questions for Rick, but they all felt that this had indeed been the Lord at work in the hearts of the people on the board at Bethany Church. They ended the lengthy conversation that evening with a time of prayer over the phone lines. They called on the Lord to work in similar ways in other churches in their regions. They prayed that this would spread to other churches and other denominations throughout America.

They would not be satisfied until this had become a nation-wide happening.

Two weeks later, Rick met again with the pastor and board of Bethany Church. As soon as he saw the pastor's face he knew that the Saturday two weeks earlier had been just the beginning of something great. As the board members came in the room, Rick noticed on each one's face a look of joy. There was almost a stunned look but it was a look of great joy and contentment.

"Well, tell me about the last two weeks," Rick said, starting the meeting. "Obviously something has been happening. I can tell just by the look on your faces. What have you been experiencing?"

"I hardly know where to start," Hank jumped in. "I didn't realize what a profound effect this was going to have on my life. I have shared my faith with seven people in my neighborhood and at work. All of them are taking it very seriously, and one has already accepted Christ. I keep praying that the others will do so also. But, you know, something else has happened that was completely unexpected. I didn't tell anyone, but my wife and I have really been having a hard time of it lately. It seems we were always fighting about nothing. Any little, unimportant thing would set us to arguing. I was wondering if we were going to survive as a couple.

"Rick, when you pointed out the selfish attitudes people have about the church and how they demand what they want in the church, it had a profound effect on my attitudes about it. I could see how selfish I have been about church. It brought me to a place of genuine repentance and sorrow for my sinful attitude. When I got home that day my wife could see a difference. She wanted to know what had happened. Well, it took me most of that afternoon and evening to relate all that had happened. I showed her all the ways I have been so selfish about the church. I explained how God had moved all of us to repentance for our sinful attitudes.

"Then something truly unexpected happened. She began to cry. I thought maybe the Lord was moving her to repentance about her selfish attitudes about the church. But, no, this was something else. She was applying what you had taught us to her attitudes about our marriage. 'Hank,' she began to cry, 'that describes what I have been like in our marriage. I have been so selfish. I wanted what I wanted without giving very much thought to what you might want. I selfishly demanded my own way instead of thinking about what would be good for us as a couple. I am so sorry for sinning against you and against God.' And you know something, Rick? I found myself going through a whole new bout of repentance. I realized I had also had a selfish attitude about our marriage. I had wanted everything the way I wanted it to be without giving much thought to what would be best for my wife. We knelt in prayer, crying out in repentance for our selfishness in our marriage and in the church. I haven't cried that much since I was a baby! But you know something? God has worked a transformation in our marriage. Oh, we still have some rough patches, but now we stop and think of the 'one flesh' unit we have become. I now realize that when I put love into my wife I am actually loving myself, because I am putting love into the 'one flesh' unit we have become. My wife and I have started a journey into something we have never experienced before. It is a journey of giving ourselves selflessly to each other and to our Lord and to his church."

"Wow, that's wonderful," Rick said. "It is wonderful when the Lord brings us to the place of genuine repentance. It affects every area of our life. Well, that one may be hard to top, but what has it been like for the rest of you?"

"Probably the biggest thing I notice is my attitude regarding the church," Phil said. "I no longer have this desperate need to be in control of things lest something bad happen. I can trust the Lord to bring about wonderful results. In fact, I can trust him a lot more than I can trust myself. I have had to face the fact that, more often than I would like to admit, I have really acted as a 'church boss.' I can also see that the church hasn't exactly thrived under my 'boss-ship,' if I can invent such a word. In fact, the church has done very poorly when I have tried to control it. Being boss brought some satisfaction to my need to be in control, but it certainly didn't bring good results for the church. Each time I drive up to the church I go through a little bit of repentance for my failings to influence the church to the Lordship of Christ, especially in the area of evangelism. And I pray for the church that God would bring all the people to the point of repentance that the Lord has brought to us on the board. It's not that I think we are superior because of this. I just long for everyone to experience the peace and joy that come from recognizing our sin and genuinely repenting of it. I also have been much more active in reaching out to my neighbors and friends. You know, it's a funny thing. When I got my attitude about the church straightened out it had an effect on my whole life. I am much more relaxed and joyful. I don't feel the need to control in other areas of my life to such a degree as before. People have noticed it and are asking me what has changed. I just beam and say the Lord has been at work in my life and in my attitudes. Their curiosity has been great enough that in several cases I have been able to share the gospel. I guess that is what you were saying a few months ago about genuine holiness being winsome, not weird. This much I know for sure. This sure is a more relaxed and happy way to live. I can just be content in trusting the Lord to do what is the very best thing without him needing my advice. He seems to be doing a whole lot better job with the church than I could ever do." He chuckled.

"All right, anyone else?" urged Rick.

"Well, you know that I am so quiet that I have a real hard time speaking up," said Betty. Rick certainly agreed with that statement. Betty had hardly said anything in all the sessions they had been through over the last few months. "The Lord has been doing something truly unusual for me," Betty continued. "He has been giving me an influence with the people of the church that I never had before. I was always so shy that I just sort of was content to follow silently. But it's different now. I am still shy, but the Lord has done something in me. He has given me a confidence I didn't have before. I guess once I admitted that I, too, had been selfish about the church it opened the door for the Lord to do some things in my life that needed doing. He has given me a confidence that can only have come from him. I don't have to be nervous around people. I can trust the Lord to do the very best thing in that situation. People have started asking me what has changed. As I explain they start asking what has been going on in those meetings the board has been having with the regional superintendent. They notice that all the people who have been in those meetings seem changed. They like the changes they are seeing, and they want to know what has been happening. I try to explain it the best I can, and it seems I get enough across that they understand at least a little of it. And, you know, a funny thing has been happening. When they hear about it they have a very positive response. They start saying, 'Our church has needed something like that. I have been so worried that Bethany Church was going to die. Maybe the Lord hasn't forgotten about us after all.' They also start to recognize that maybe they have been part of the problem themselves. I think some of them might be ready to face the truth about their part in bringing the church to the point of near death. Maybe God will spread what we experienced to the church as a whole. Do you think that could happen, Rick?"

"I sure do," Rick said. "We need to be really praying that the Lord will bring this about."

"Pastor, what has been your experience of the last few weeks?" Rick inquired. Rick was surprised when he saw the pastor beginning to tear up in response to his question.

"This has really spoken to me," began the pastor. "I have been praying about this for so long. Now I realize that I have been part of the problem myself. I allowed myself to become hard of heart. After so many times when people have come against me out of their own selfishness, I had just about given up. I found myself erecting a protective shell around myself. I wasn't going to let anyone hurt me again. I found myself trying to control the church to prevent myself from getting hurt. I was using the church for my own selfish ends. No wonder my leadership wasn't as effective as it had been in years past. After our time of repentance together, God has broken down that protective shell. I have found myself being much more approachable again. People in the church are noticing it and drawing closer to me. But, wonder of wonders, my next door neighbor has noticed a change. He has been hanging around me more, and the most wonderful thing happened. Yesterday I was able to lead him to faith in Christ! What a tremendous experience. He says he wants to start attending church this Sunday. He even wants to be baptized. Won't that be something special?

"And you know what else? I think this is starting to have an effect on many more people in our church. They are noticing how the board members have changed and, strangely enough, are starting to say, 'I want that for myself too!' I think they are getting ready for the Lord to do something powerful in their lives as well."

"That brings me to one last thing I want us to learn together," Rick said. "Let's pick up on this after a short break."

QUESTIONS FOR REFLECTION

1. According to this book, what might the members of your church need to repent of? What might you need to repent of?

2. What would your church look like if there was genuine repentance and an awakening of the church? How would it be different?

PRAYER

"**I THINK THERE ARE MANY THINGS WE CAN BE DOING TO SPREAD THIS THROUGHOUT OUR CHURCH AND OUR NATION," RICK BEGAN AFTER THE BREAK.** "But I think the most important thing we can do is pray. We talked about this before, but I want to reemphasize it today. We need to be praying that God would work powerfully to bring about repentance and brokenness on the part of many people in this congregation and throughout our nation. Actually, what we should be praying for is that the Lord would bring brokenness and repentance to *all* the people in this church and in *every* church around this country. Only the Lord can bring about the great awakening the church so desperately needs in America. We cannot make it happen. It will happen only if the Lord brings about a great movement of the Holy Spirit in the lives of many people. We cannot bring that about ourselves. We cannot manufacture a great awakening, and we dare not try to manipulate such a thing. We are utterly dependent on the holy One to bring this about. All of the things I have taught you are going to become very important if, or maybe I should say when, the Lord brings about a generalized awakening of his people in America. We will need to make sure that churches understand how to effectively reach lost people and begin to put in place the practices to bring that about. But things have to come in order. If we don't have, first, a movement of the Holy Spirit among millions of Christians similar to what we experienced, we will not see the desired results. Just as with us, there needs to come a point of recognition on the part of millions of Christians that they have been killing the church with their selfish attitudes. They need to have their eyes opened to the fact that the church doesn't exist to entertain, pamper, coddle them, or stroke their egos. The main reason the church exists on earth today is to bring lost people to a saving knowledge of faith in Jesus.

"God, and only God, can bring this about. But he has chosen to work through people. He has chosen to work through those who can teach effectively on this, and he has asked us to pray diligently for him to work to bring this about. He has asked us to pray fervently that he would bring forth laborers for the fields, which are white unto harvest. He could make this happen without our prayers. But he has chosen to work through our prayers. Sometimes we don't fully understand this, but we know it is true. Only the Lord can break through to the stubborn hearts of people who have been in the church for generations and think it is their private little fiefdom. Only he can re-educate those who have been trained to think that their job as church members is to consume the services that the church is obligated to provide. Only the Lord can transform consumers into warriors. But, and this is important to remember, he has chosen to work through our prayers and our labors. He will use us in this process of bringing about a great awakening if we stay close to him, if we pray fervently, and if we speak by our words and our life into the lives of people who have bought the lies of Satan. They have been deceived, but the Lord can use us to bring light and power into their lives. It all starts with prayer. Probably there is nothing you can do at this exact time that is more important than prayer. I urge you to pray fervently and to recruit others to pray for this also. Small groups of prayer warriors would be a great idea. But be careful that the evil one does not hijack these times of prayer for the awakening of the church and turn them into the usual prayer meetings. You know, the ones where the most important thing we pray about is Aunt Mary's hang nail! We have much bigger fish to fry than that!

"Do you have any questions about any of this?" Rick asked.

"Do you think this puts us on the front lines of spiritual warfare?" inquired Hank.

"It sure does," Rick replied.

"Well isn't that a little dangerous?" said Hank. "I mean, won't we come under the attack of Satan? Can't he make our lives a little miserable? What should we be doing about that?"

Rick responded, "Yes, Hank, you are absolutely right about this. When we begin to pose a threat to Satan's control over people's lives, both within and outside of the church, he certainly will attack back. But remember the promise we are given in First John 4:4, 'You, dear children, are from God and have overcome them, because the one who is in you is greater than the one who is in the world.' Through Jesus Christ who lives within us we have authority over Satan and the demons. That does not mean that we can safely be ignorant of his schemes. Even though we have authority over Satan and the demons, and even though we as Christians cannot be demon possessed, we can still allow ourselves to be influenced by him. That is why the Scriptures tell us to be alert to his schemes. In 1 Peter 5:7-9 it says, 'Cast all your anxiety on him because he cares for you. Be self-controlled and alert. Your enemy the devil prowls around like a roaring lion looking for someone to devour. Resist him, standing firm in the faith, because you know that your brothers throughout the world are undergoing the same kind of sufferings.' We are told to be alert. These words are addressed to Christians. If Satan could have no influence on us, these words would be unnecessary. We are to resist Satan. That involves standing firm in the faith. We are to remind ourselves and each other of the truths of Scripture so that we don't succumb to his devious ways. The written word of God is the best defense against the influence of Satan. Even Jesus quoted Scripture each time he was tempted by the devil in the wilderness. Know the Bible. Study it, memorize it, and meditate on it. That is your greatest defense against Satan's schemes. That is why we are instructed in Colossians 3:1-3, 'Since, then, you have been raised with Christ, set your hearts on things above, where Christ is seated at the right hand of God. Set your minds on things above, not on earthly things. For you died, and your life is now hidden with Christ in God.' Keep thinking about what God's will for the church really is. Keep praying for the awakening of the church. Don't let yourself get bogged down with the cares of this world."

"Well what should we be looking out for?" Cindy asked.

"Here are some of Satan's favorite schemes," Rick said. "He will work through discouragement. You may get tired from the strenuous nature of this work. Satan loves to approach a tired Christian and whisper words like, 'This isn't working so well is it? You must be a pretty wimpy Christian if you are getting so tired. Just look at Bill. He still has that same selfish attitude about the church, and he seems so happy and carefree.' Remember, this is warfare. You are going to get tired. That doesn't mean there is anything wrong with you or that God has failed you. It just means you are in warfare and you are going to get tired!

"Another favorite place for Satan to attack is through our marriages or our children. The spouses and children of people who are on the front lines face more attacks than the spouses and children of complacent Christians. Satan doesn't need to attack them. They are already ineffective and represent no threat to his kingdom. Be sensitive to discouragement and bad attitudes on the part of your spouse and children, and pray for them. Be kind to them. They are coming under greater attack. It may even show up in the form of nightmares or disturbed sleep. Satan has limited power in this world, but he may even affect your health or theirs. But that can be overcome through prayer."

Ahh, a thought struck Rick. *That explains why Al's son is having such a hard time accepting the truth. Satan is misleading him to get at Al to discourage him.*

"Satan often attacks us through our thoughts. He whispers in our ears thoughts that thoroughly distract us from the cause of Christ. Often he gives thoughts that lead to self-pity or depression. Learn to recognize that those thoughts are from him. We are commanded in 1 Thessalonians 5:16-18, 'Be joyful always; pray continually; give thanks in all circumstances, for this is God's will for you in Christ Jesus.' If we are thinking self-pitying thoughts, we are letting Satan win the battle for our thoughts. If we are not rejoicing always and giving thanks in all circumstances, then we are giving in to the evil one. We know that God is at work in all of our circumstances and will bring good out of them in his perfect way and time. It is up to us to choose to be thankful no matter what our circumstances. If we are not being thankful it is proof positive that our thoughts are not the way the Lord wants them to be and the way he empowers us to be. He never commands us to do anything that he does not also give us the power to do. If we have been given a command, we know we also have been given the power to obey it. It is up to us to access that power and obey that command. This isn't overlooking the fact that some people have chemical imbalances that require that they be on anti-depressant medications. That is really no different than if they had diabetes and needed to be on insulin. But even they, along with using their medicine, need to be choosing to rejoice always and be thankful in every circumstance. Be very alert to each other. Anytime you notice one of your fellow board members who seem to be discouraged or suffering in any way, jump in to pray for them and gently guide their thoughts to be on the things of the Lord. Colossians 3:2 tells us to set our minds on things above, not on earthly things. That doesn't mean we can be oblivious to the experiences of real life. It means that our focus is first to be on the Lord and what He is doing in our lives and the lives of others.

"One thing becomes very clear," Rick continued. "We need to be praying for each other. We know that those of us who have gone through this experience and are putting ourselves on the front lines of this battle will come under greater attack. Pray fervently for each other. Don't just sit idly by while the evil one attacks one of your brothers or sisters in this battle. And also remember that the Christians who are still living complacent, consumer-oriented Christian lives are not the enemy. They are victims of the enemy. Pray that the Lord would wake them up also. Pray that they will see the light and repent of their sinful attitudes and their disobedience. Pray for the church throughout America, and actually throughout the world. But the church in America is especially in need of an awakening. Pray for that day to come and come soon. This is a time in the history of the church where prayer is one of the most important things we can do. Let's be about the labor of prayer.

"Any other questions?" Rick asked.

"Well, you answered my question pretty thoroughly," Phil said. "I was going to ask what we do next, but you have given me the most important part of the answer. Pray fervently!"

"Yes, that is the most important part," Rick said. "But there is more we can do. Look for every opportunity to share with others the things you have learned about why the church is in such a sad state in America and what it is going to take to get it on a much better path. Don't force it down their throats; listen carefully to them to discern how much they want to hear. Be alert to any positive responses. The Lord may use you in small ways to lead people to awakening one by one. Don't overlook the power of that possibility. Enough "one by ones" and the whole church will be significantly affected by the transformation of individuals. Well, let's call it a day. But, before we do, let's spend some time in prayer together for each other, for Bethany Church, and for Christians around the nation."

Without any prompting, the people knelt by their chairs and began to pray with great energy. Rick had never seen a church board praying like this. These folks truly believed that God and God alone could bring about the longed for changes in the churches. It was clear that there was a determination in their voices and in their actions. They were determined to be used by God to make a difference in His work in the world.

QUESTIONS FOR REFLECTION

1. Am I praying for the repentance and awakening of the church?

2. Since Satan does not want churches to be awakened, what might spiritual warfare look like in your congregation and in your life personally?

THE BEGINNING OF THE END, OR THE END OF THE BEGINNING?

RICK FOUND HIMSELF PRETTY TIRED AS HE DROVE HOME FROM THIS MEETING. Well, that is putting it too mildly. He was actually exhausted. It had been a long few months getting to this point. But, what a point to come to! Rick was thrilled with all that had happened. He hoped and prayed that this was the beginning of something wonderful happening in Bethany Church and in many churches in his region and throughout America. He hoped passionately that this would not be the end of what God was doing. He hoped that things at Bethany Church would not just fizzle out and die, leaving the church to go back to the way things had always been. He hoped that Bethany Church was not the end of this movement of the Holy Spirit in the lives of believers. His prayer was that this would be spread to many churches in his region and throughout the nation.

Rick, Al, and Wayne were able to get together for a day at the end of that month to compare notes, pray together, and strategize for what to do next. They all had a profound sense that this wasn't just a matter of their own wisdom and strategies. They all realized that what had happened at Bethany Church was a movement of God, not just the result of their own efforts. But they also realized that God had chosen to use them as his servants in bringing this about. They so wanted to make sure they were doing all they could do to be used further. They wanted to see so much more happening than what they had seen up to this point. One after the other they began to pray, starting with Al, "Lord, thank you for the privilege of being your servants in this great undertaking. What a joy it is to see you at work in such a powerful way. Thank you for starting to answer the prayers we have been praying for so long. I confess that I have had moments of growing weary in this long process. Thank you for forgiving me for all my sins and for continuing to use a weak and sin prone person like me. Lord, I pray that this is not the end of all that you want to accomplish among your people. I know it isn't. I know that you want to awaken all your people in our churches and in the whole land. Lord, we can't do that in our own strength, but we know that you are not limited to our strength. You give supernatural power to each of us and you work beyond our efforts. Lord, I pray, let us have a small part in what you are going to do among your people. I pray, work powerfully in the hearts of Christians throughout America. Bring your people to the point of repentance that we saw happening with the Christians at Bethany Church."

Wayne followed, "Lord, we know that this battle is going to get intense. The evil one is not going to take this lying down. He will fight back with all the resources he can marshal. He will especially attack our spouses and children. In fact, that probably explains why Al's son Matt has chosen to not believe in the truths of the Scriptures. Satan has been influencing him in an attempt to neutralize Al in this struggle. You know how precious our children are to us. You know how it hurts us when one of them suffers. I pray, protect Al against discouragement regarding his son. Protect him against the words of the deceiver as he tries to whisper in his ear, 'What kind of father are you anyway? Your own son doesn't believe in God. How do you think you can be a servant of God when your own son doesn't believe? What business do you have leading churches when your own family isn't in order? Surely God won't use you in any significant way to bring awakening to his people when your own son is in need of an awakening.' Lord, protect Rick's wife from any more physical attacks. Bring complete healing to her body in the months after her surgery. Give her the diligence to complete all the physical therapy recommended in her case. Strengthen her. Lord, strengthen all of our wives and children during this time. We know they will come under special attack from Satan. Protect them and give them wisdom to be alert to his schemes. Give them wisdom to stand firm against his efforts. Give them strength to rejoice always, pray continuously, and give thanks in all circumstances. But, above all, we pray, move powerfully among the people in our churches and throughout our nation. Please bring the great awakening the church in this country so desperately needs."

It was Rick's turn, and he began, "Oh, Lord, thank you for beginning to answer the prayers we have been praying for so long. Please let this be a beginning of something much greater than what we have seen so far. Lord, protect those folks at Bethany Church who have responded to the challenges I gave them on your behalf. We know Satan will attack them severely in an attempt to stop this whole movement in its tracks. Give them wisdom to see Satan's schemes for what they really are, and give them strength to choose to trust in you and rejoice in you rather than succumbing to discouragement. I beseech you to spread this movement of the Holy Spirit throughout Bethany Church. Lord, speak to the hearts of many more people within that congregation, and draw them to repentance for the selfish and consumer-oriented approach to church that they have been following. Lord, bring an awakening to Bethany Church that can stand as an example to many churches around this nation. And, Lord, give wisdom to Al, Wayne, and to me as we seek to be your servants in this great cause, the awakening of the church in America. I pray for Al's son, Matt. Lord, break through the confusion Satan has placed in his heart and mind. Clear up the truth for him so that he understands your great love for him and for all people. Lord, I'm going to go out on a limb here and ask that you would reclaim him for yourself and empower him in a special way. I ask specifically that you would choose him to be a leader in the movement of awakening churches and Christians throughout this once great land of ours. Use him, I pray. Lord, here we are, three weak and fallible men. But you can use us. You have typically chosen those who were not recognized as great by the world. Please use us to accomplish your purposes in the churches of this land. In the name of your Son, our Savior, Jesus Christ, we pray. Amen."

"Well, what do we do next?" Al said.

"God has promised to guide us, and he has already used us in a beginning sort of way," Rick said. "I keep having the feeling that I should start addressing the whole congregation at Bethany Church. Who knows? Maybe the Lord will work in the whole congregation in a similar way. Meanwhile let's keep praying that the Lord will give you two some opportunities to speak to the boards of some churches in your regions also. Our deep longing is to see this happen over and over again in the churches in our regions. We know that the Lord wants this to happen. Let's pray to that end and seek every opportunity we can to extend what we have seen the Lord do already. Why don't we talk in a month and see what the Lord has done in each of our situations by then?"

The guys agreed on the strategy and promised to be praying for each other. They even had time to watch the Colorado and Nebraska football game together. Too bad Colorado got whomped by Nebraska again. Rick had to take his share of not-so-gentle humor over that, but the guys had gotten to know each other so well that it was all in good fun. Besides, these things just didn't matter so much anymore. Their hearts were afire with something far more important.

Later that week Rick called the pastor at Bethany Church.

"I've been wondering," Rick said. "Would it be wise if we would take some deliberate steps to speak to the rest of your congregation? Maybe the Lord would choose to use us to lead the whole congregation to a similar point of repentance to what we have experienced."

"I've been praying about the exact same thing," the pastor responded. "What do you have in mind?"

"Why don't you and I tag-team on this?" Rick suggested. "I think it is important for the congregation to see that you are fully on board with this. They will be less likely to see me as just some 'hired gun' from the outside if you are doing some of the teaching on this subject. Have you given any thought to which of the subjects I covered you would most like to do the preaching on?"

"Well, it would be best if I did not do the one on following pastoral leadership," was the pastor's first remark. "It will seem way less self-serving if you cover that one. But I would love to do the teaching on the consumer mentality and how we will need to see a radical restructuring of Christians' values if the church is going to become effective once again. I have talked with the board about doing this, and they are in full agreement with what we are talking about today. They are eager to see this grow beyond just them."

Rick and the pastor talked it over and agreed on who would teach what and when they would start this series of messages to the whole congregation. They agreed that there was no value in waiting, so they planned to start this teaching series in two weeks with Rick covering the condition of the church in America today.

"Let's really be in prayer before we start this. Have all the board members in prayer about this also," Rick urged. "There is so much at stake here. The consequences can reach far beyond just Bethany Church."

Rick couldn't wait for a month to talk to his buddies about this. He called them up to ask for their prayers for the situation. Al was really excited, himself. The board of Hope Church had asked him to come lead them through some strategizing about the future of the church. Hope Church was in a rather steep decline, and the board members had become honest enough with themselves to face this fact and realize they needed help. He would start meeting with them next Saturday. He asked for the others to be praying for him as he launched into this project. Wayne was still floating feelers out to churches to see if any of them were interested in help turning their congregations around. So far no opportunity had surfaced. The three friends prayed together on the phone that the Lord would use each of them in the ways that were being presented. They promised to continue praying for each other over the next two weeks.

When Rick brought to Bethany Church the message about the condition of the church in America, it elicited a lot of sad shaking of heads and mumbled assent to the facts. These people had seen enough to know that things were not good. They just did not know how bad it really was. Once they heard the reality it was very sobering for them. But how could things be any different? They were just like a whole lot of other churches in the same boat. In one way they didn't feel so bad, but in another they were really scared by the truth of the condition of the church. It was a very sober congregation that morning as Rick concluded his message. He did promise them, however, that this wasn't the end. There was hope for the church. He let them know that in the next few weeks the pastor and he would share the reasons for this decline and what it would take for this to turn around. He asked the congregation to begin praying for this time in the life of Bethany Church and to be praying for churches around the nation.

The next Sunday the pastor began his message, "I want to share something with you this morning that has been on my heart for over twenty years." Rick was surprised at the strength and passion with which he was speaking. This had obviously been a deep concern of his. "Something has bothered me for a long time," he continued, "but I didn't fully understand what it was or what to do about it until our regional superintendent, Rick, explained to our board what is happening to churches in America. Now I can put words to what has been such a deep concern of mine for so long." He went on to explain in strong but loving words the problem with the consumer orientation of most Christians in America. As Rick watched him preach and scanned the congregation, he began to pray fervently, if silently. He could see glimpses of recognition on the faces of some of the people, but he could also see some anger on the faces of others. They had spent their whole lives living one way in the church and had grown very comfortable with that way. As they listened to their pastor laying bare the carnal motives behind their comfort-seeking style of doing church, it scared them. They reacted like a child would react if you pulled their toy away from them. Rick was afraid that some of them were just minutes away from erupting in anger. The pastor stayed strong through the whole message, even though he obviously was seeing the same facial expressions that Rick was seeing. As he concluded, it was a silent congregation that filed out of the church that morning. A few gathered in groups talking. Some of them were clearly angry about what had been said that morning. Rick began to wonder what would happen as a result of his meddling in this congregation.

As he and the pastor met in the pastor's office, the pastor remained resolute. "If it costs me my job, then so be it. I can't just sit here and watch the church dying around me anymore. Let's press forward and ask the Lord to overcome the resistance we are obviously seeing on the faces of some of the folks this morning."

Just then, four of the board members knocked on the door to the office. As they entered, they embraced the pastor.

"Pastor, we said we would be with you all the way. Now a few arrows are starting to fly your way. We are not going to desert you," Hank remarked. "We are standing right here beside you and Rick. We will not give up on this. This is spiritual warfare, and, of course, there are going to be some skirmishes. We can't expect anything less. Let's pray together right now."

All six of them knelt by the chairs in the office and began to call on the almighty Lord of heaven and earth to intervene. They passionately called on the Lord to work in the hearts of the people of the congregation. They asked him to do the work of softening hard hearts. They called on the Lord to calm the fears of those who were just afraid of losing the church as they had always known it. They beseeched the Lord to bring a spiritual awakening to this congregation and to many more throughout America. Rick was so pleased to see the steadfastness of these who had been led by the Lord through him to a place of spiritual life.

"We have to expect some resistance," Rick said, encouraging them. "If there was no resistance, I would question if we were really clarifying the issue in the people's minds. This is a battle between Christ and Satan. Let's keep on fighting and keep on trusting the Lord to bring a breakthrough."

As everyone left the room after this prayer session, they promised to keep praying diligently the whole week.

The next Sunday morning, Rick launched into the message on how the church had so seriously failed to fulfill the command of the Lord to reach as many lost people as they could possibly reach. He noticed that some of the people who had seemed most angry at last Sunday's message were not there this Sunday. There seemed to be less resistance as he preached. People really seemed to be getting the point as he bored in on how they substitute anything and everything for obedience to Christ on this matter. They seemed to understand that evangelism must be the number one priority of the church and how the church would simply cease to exist if it was not. They certainly saw plenty of evidence of that fact all around them. Their church was dying for lack of commitment to evangelism. He could see a creeping sadness on the faces of the people as they realized how badly they had failed to do the will of God on this matter. A sober congregation filed out that morning after the service concluded, but Rick did not see any groups of angry people in the foyer this day. The few most vociferous ring leaders seemed to have stayed away from this service. He wondered if maybe one of them might have been a "church boss" type. The pastor later confirmed that was the case.

In the ensuing weeks, Rick and the pastor continued to teach the congregation about why churches are dying. When they got to the messages about what needs to change for churches to become alive and healthy again, the mood seemed to become more positive. Gradually looks of despair were being replaced by expressions of hope.

The resistance had seemed to steadily lower each Sunday, although it temporarily spiked up again on the Sunday about cultural relevancy. Some of these folks had been rather adamant about not accepting "that new music." But Rick felt that, in spite of their discomfort, they were comprehending the truth of what he was saying, and it was a short-lived resistance. By the end of the message, most seemed to have accepted that they were going to have to make some changes.

On the Sunday that the pastor taught about the need to take risks there were also some fearful looks. These people had operated in the safety zone all their lives. This idea of deliberately starting to walk by faith was unsettling. But by now, most of them had accepted that there would be some changes coming. Even when Rick taught about a radical restructuring of Christians' values they seemed accepting. It seemed that they were facing reality and embracing the idea of change.

Rick heard from Al that things were not going so well at Hope Church. Some of the board members were just digging in their heels at the things he was teaching them. After a few weeks of this, Al had concluded that it was a waste of time going any further with them. He had asked to discontinue his time of meeting with them, and some of them had seemed very relieved. He had begun to suspect that one of them was really the "church boss" and didn't want to lose his power. Al had closed the door on that experience with great sadness. It appeared as if Hope Church was going to choose to stay on the path to the death of the congregation. Al let them know that he would continue to pray for them that some of what he had said to them would begin to sink in.

The next Sunday Rick began to preach at Bethany Church about the need for repentance. He emphasized that until they recognized how badly they had failed the Lord in obeying the Great Commission, the Lord wouldn't work in a powerful way. As he preached, an amazing thing began to happen. One person after another began to wipe their eyes. Some began shaking with sobs. He continued on with what he had to say. By the time he was done, many were openly crying.

He ended by saying, "If the Lord is speaking to you in a special way today, if you are already repenting of your sins of complacency, consumer orientation, and failure to obey the Great Commission, please come to the front of the church and kneel in prayer."

Soon not only the front of the church but the aisles as well were full of people crying and praying. They were confessing their sins and asking for the Lord to work in power in their midst. It seemed as if no one wanted to go home that day. They were just hanging around, hugging each other, confessing sins to each other, and praying for each other.

Rick was wary of the fact that this could be just an emotional experience. He didn't want this to degenerate into just an emotional high like some of the recent attempts at revival had done. He knew that if this were the real thing it would show in some solid changes in these people's lives over the next week. He prayed that it would be so. When most of the people had finally left the church building, he and the pastor met with the members of the board in the office. They all agreed that this seemed to be the real thing and committed themselves to praying earnestly over the next week.

The next Sunday, Rick stood up to preach and was amazed at the change he saw in the faces of the people. There was a joy and contentment he had never seen on the faces of a whole congregation. Rick exhorted them to begin the work of praying for wisdom to put the changes he had been talking about into the practice of Bethany Church. He encouraged them to be praying for other congregations. He taught them that they were entering the battle of spiritual warfare and would need to be alert to the strategies of Satan. They would need to continue the good fight and let the Lord do great things among them.

Over the next two months, Rick began to hear very encouraging reports from Bethany Church. The pastor was preaching with a new authority, and the people were following his leadership. Many friends and neighbors had come to faith through the personal witness of the people, and the church was making significant changes to become more culturally relevant. They had started a number of ministries designed to meet the real needs of people outside of the church. An awakening really had occurred at Bethany Church! Rick prayed that it would continue and that the church would not just slip back into doing business as usual.

There were small, encouraging, reports from the other regional superintendents. Wayne was beginning to lead the board at one of his churches through this process, and they were responding positively. Al had actually been invited back by the board of Hope Church. It seemed as if they were finally facing the desperate condition of their church and acknowledging that something had to be done, even if it meant major changes must occur. The one man Al had suspected of being a church boss had resigned from the board and left the church. Al was looking forward to taking up where he had left off. He asked the others to pray that he would experience a different result this time.

Over the next year, the three of them had an increasing number of opportunities to lead church boards through this process with mixed results. Some of the boards had experienced a full awakening like Bethany Church had. Some others seemed to dip their toes into the water but never jumped all the way in. The three of them were slightly encouraged but hungry for more. They gathered during the week between Christmas and New Year's again for a time of prayer and strategy.

Rick began to pray, "Lord, is this all that you are going to do? We are thrilled by what happened at Bethany Church, but we long to see that spreading to many more congregations. Isn't that what you want also? We beseech you, Lord, bring awakening to Christians and churches all through this once great land. We ask you to do this before it requires a great persecution to wake up your people and purify the church. Lord, show us what to do. We want to be used as your servants in this process. But we know that what we can do is very limited. Unless you work powerfully in the hearts of Christians throughout this land, our efforts will be a pittance in a land of such great need. Please, Lord, we pray, act powerfully to bring a great awakening to your church! We will continue to pound on the gates of heaven as you have instructed us to be persistent in prayer. Lord, awaken the Christians throughout America."

The others poured out their hearts in prayer in a similar way.

As they drove away from that meeting, all three of them had such mixed emotions. They were exhilarated by the wonderful things they saw happening in a few churches. But they had a deep hunger within them to see many more churches and Christians similarly affected. They were not satisfied. They ached to see more happening. They would not be satisfied until this became a nation-wide movement of the Holy Spirit in the lives of God's people. They vowed to keep praying, and they wondered what would happen next. They desperately hoped that what they had seen so far would not be the end.

QUESTIONS FOR REFLECTION

1. If genuine repentance occurs in your congregation, what will need to change for it to be effective in reaching un-churched people? What steps can the church begin to take now?

2. How important is it to you personally that the church experience an awakening?

WEEK SIX
STUDY GUIDE

1. Have the group discuss together the statement, "If you want to build a ship, don't drum up the men to gather wood, divide the work, and give orders. Instead, teach them to yearn for the vast and endless sea." How does it apply to the current situation of the church?

2. Have the group discuss together the things that the members of the church might need to repent of.

3. Have the individuals in the group answer for themselves the question: Are there any ways that I, personally, am under spiritual attack currently or recently? Report back to the group as a whole.

4. Break into groups of three or four and discuss how they can help each other and the church as a whole to win in spiritual warfare. Report back to the group as a whole.

5. Have the group as a whole discuss what the church would look like if there was genuine repentance and an awakening of the church. How would it be different?

6. Break into groups of three or four and spend a concentrated time of prayer for the awakening of the church, for repentance to occur among the members of the church, and for the upcoming service of repentance.

HOW TO USE THE STUDY GUIDE

THE MOST EFFECTIVE WAY TO USE THIS BOOK AND STUDY GUIDE IS TO FOLLOW THE CONCLUSION OF THIS ALL-CHURCH STUDY WITH A CHURCH CONSULTATION NO MORE THAN SIXTY DAYS AFTER THE COMPLETION OF THE STUDY!

If your church cannot have a consultation but you are willing to very carefully follow the directions on how to use this study guide in your congregation, it still can have a powerful impact on your church. The study guide is included within this book so that churches can study the book together. It is my prayer that churches will have their small groups, Sunday school classes, ministry teams, and all other groups within the church studying this book simultaneously so the whole congregation will experience the impact at the same time.

Each session is designed to be completed in one weekly group meeting. All groups in the congregation should meet weekly for the six weeks of this study time together as a congregation. The groups should stay synchronized in their study of the material, completing each study session on the same week as all the other groups. The group study sessions should be about one and a half hours in length. Study group leaders will need to be at least one week ahead to prepare materials needed for each week's study.

There are also questions for reflection for the individual reader to complete at the end of each chapter. These are separate from the group study questions and should be completed by the reader before the group study meeting.

The ideal way to use this book is for the church to follow this study with a church consultation very soon after the completion of this study. It should actually be scheduled before the study is begun so that within two months after finishing the study, the consultation will be completed. If that is not going to be done, then the following steps should be taken:

After session six, schedule an all-church service of repentance for our disobedience to the Lord in fulfilling the Great Commission. The pastor should preach on the state of the church in America today and why it has gotten to the dismal state it is in. He should strongly call the church to repentance and urge the members to make some physical statement of repentance such as coming to the front of the church for prayers of repentance, or standing up in place as a show of genuine repentance.

The next Sunday the pastor may want to preach on some of the specific changes the church will need to make to become effective in its outreach to un-churched people.

After this, the pastor should begin to work with the board of the church to establish specific changes, ministries, and strategies to become effective in reaching un-churched people.

Before you implement the specific changes, lead your congregation to celebrate its past history. One idea is to place a long strip of newsprint or butcher paper along the wall of the church or fellowship hall. Divide it into decades of the church history and have the members write on the paper what they thought were significant events in the decades both for the church as a whole and for them as individuals.

Have a service or banquet of celebrating the past before plunging into the future. Have members share their special memories. Sing favorite songs. Sing songs of praise. Make it a time of fond memories. Then end the service by clearly closing the door on the past, stepping into the new plan for the future, and figuratively speaking, lead the congregation into the new future.

To schedule a consultation, please contact Dr. Meyer at 303-290-9083, or robert-meyer@msn.com. If his schedule does not permit him to do the consultation himself, he has a number of qualified consultants who can do this work on his behalf.

ENDNOTES

1 David Olson. *The American Church in Crisis*. Grand Rapids: Zondervan, 2008

2 Dan Schafer. *Spiritual Fathers, Restoring the Reproductive Church*. Littleton: Building Brothers

3 Schafer. *Spiritual Fathers*

4 Shiloh Place Ministries. Information drawn from Focus on the Family, MinistriesToday, Charisma Magazine, TNT Ministries, and other respected groups.

5 George Barna. *The Second Coming of the Church*. Nashville: Word, 2001

BIBLIOGRAPHY

Olson, David. *The American Church in Crisis*. Grand Rapids: Zondervan, 2008

Schafer, Dan. *Spiritual Fathers, Restoring the Reproductive Church*. Littleton: Building Brothers

Shiloh Place Ministries. Information drawn from Focus on the Family, MinistriesToday, Charisma Magazine, TNT Ministries, and other respected groups.

Barna, George. *The Second Coming of the Church*. Nashville: Word, 2001